MARKED
BY
AZURITE

CELINE JEANJEAN

ISBN: 9782492523267

Cover by: bonobobookcovers.com
Editing by: copybykath.com

JOIN MY NEWSLETTER

AND RECEIVE THESE FREE STORIES

Subscribe to Celine Jeanjean's newsletter and receive these
three novellas for free!
Go to:
http://celinejeanjean.com

1

I accept the drink from Chai without the shudder of dread that normally accompanies receiving one of his cocktails. That's because he hasn't made this one, so my tastebuds and stomach are safe. We're sitting at the counter of the Scarlet Lounge, enjoying a drink on one of my rare nights off from the barbershop.

I take a sip. Thai-chili-infused tequila, Szechuan aloe syrup, fresh lime juice, and agave nectar. Just the right amount of tartness, and when I sip from the glass, the szechuan-salt rim tingles my lips.

Delish.

Chai frowns at his drink. "I'd have done it differently, myself."

I refrain from suggesting that any changes he'd make would undoubtedly turn this from a delicious drink to a stomach-curdling concoction. Chai's a fantastic sculptor, a great artist, and it's one of life's great mysteries that he's unable to realise just how vile his cocktails are. He gets such joy from his cocktail making that I let him torture my tastebuds regularly without telling him my true opinion. What else is friendship for?

I'll come clean the day he decides to make a cocktail for one of his clients, though. Luckily he decided a long time ago that his public artist persona only drinks and serves champagne or whiskey when clients come to his studio. "Classic and timeless, just like my work, darling," he told me when I asked about it.

I take another sip, looking at the bar around me. It's the kind of place that screams 'poser'. The chairs are large and vintage, upholstered in velvet and tufted. The tables are made out of pallets and painted in garish, neon colours. Paintings in gilded frames hang from the ceiling. Lights are nestled inside champagne coupes that also dangle from the ceiling, upside down, the coupe acting like a glass lampshade of sorts.

The other patrons are mostly hipsters. Spray-on jeans, vintage black felt sombreros, eyeliner – and that's just the men. A disturbing number of people are wearing sunglasses indoors. At night.

Tossers.

And no, the leather, fingerless gloves I'm wearing aren't my attempt at fashion or style. Instead, I have to keep them on to hide the silver glowing beneath the skin of my left hand, from when I freed Sarroch from Nerong's silver cage.

The Scarlet Lounge is the kind of place I normally avoid like the plague. I'm much more partial to rundown old man pubs, or jazz dives. They feel real, authentic—the sticky floor underfoot as much a part of the experience as the jazz trumpet soloist on the stage. The Scarlet Lounge tries far too hard to be cool and arty to achieve either.

The only thing I like is a large copper sculpture of vines at the edge of the bar. Delicate copper strands run up a pillar, reaching the ceiling and fanning out into a metallic canopy. It looks remarkably realistic, and the detail is incredible. If I wasn't so familiar with Chai's work, I might think he had done it.

It's far too tasteful for the joint, and it clashes with the very average cantopop that blares through the speakers. "The owner has piss poor taste in music," I comment, taking another sip. At least the drinks are good.

"Cantopop is all the rage, these days. You only think that because you're twenty-seven going on seventy," Chai teases.

"The older generations are wise and should be respected, and with good reason. They actually had good taste in music."

"Not everything after the nineteen fifties is rubbish."

"I like plenty of new stuff," I protest. "So long as it's jazz, rock 'n' roll, blues, swing," I add with a wink. "That synthetic stuff is just noise for teenyboppers to use as background music for their selfie videos."

Chai laughs. "Spoken like a true granny. Dismissing an entire generation as irrelevant."

I nod. "Yep. When I'm old enough, I'll make such a great curmudgeon. Bring on old age, I say. But anyway, why are we here? I know this isn't your kind of place, any more than it is mine. It's far too pretentious."

"It is, darling, but as you know pretentious is my bread-and-butter."

"You want to sell them a sculpture?"

He nods. "Of course. I'm born and bred Panongian, and hipsters do love things that are locally produced. Plus, I'm gay, so I get to tick that all-important diversity box. And then of course there are my all important anti-patriarchy essays to explain the meaning of my pieces."

I grin. "You can pretend all you want, I know you're a feminist at heart."

"Amen, sister. Course I am. But if there are pretentious idiots who want to pay me extra for spouting pompous stuff at them, I damn well will. I've got the older business man market quite well sewn-up, and now I want to go after the hot young type of clients."

"Do hot young things buy sculptures?"

"When Daddy is a Chinese billionaire, they do."

"There are Chinese billionaires here?" I ask dubiously, glancing around me.

"No. But getting my pieces in bars considered hot and trendy in Panong will help me get into hot and trendy bars in Hong Kong. And then Shanghai. And *there* one can find numerous trust fund babies looking to spend Daddy's billions." Chai looks around. "I'm thinking my Misericordia would be a good fit here. What do you think, petal?"

It would fit, but something else is tugging on my attention, distracting me. It's not just all the pretentiousness of the place, something doesn't feel quite right.

I tell Chai as much.

He smiles widely. "I knew you'd pick up on it! I knew you'd sniff it out like some adorable, pink-haired bloodhound. There is protection in place to keep it hidden, of course, but..."

The moment Chai mentions the word protection, I reach out with my magic. I feel it at once. In fact, it's so powerful I'm amazed I didn't get slapped in the face with it as soon as I walked into the joint.

Magic is leaking everywhere, and the air is so thick with it, it's almost like a perfume, cloying and sickly. Now that I've picked up on it, I can feel it buzzing against my skin, like the feeling you get when you lick a battery, except all over my body.

"But we didn't transition into a Mayak space," I whisper to Chai. "Did we? Did I miss it?"

He shakes his head. "This is rumoured to be the first Mayak bar set up in the Mundane reality. That's why I didn't warn you ahead of time, I wanted to see if you would pick up on it all by yourself. You know how I'm rubbish at sensing magic—I can't sense anything."

"Do the Mundanes know about it?"

"Not as far as I know. It's supposed to be a 'regular' bar."

I'm still amazed that I didn't pick up on the magic straightaway. The protection spells are obviously only designed to hide the magic from the Mundanes, and they would have worked on me so long as I didn't use my magic, since I'm human. At least I'm pretty sure I am.

Looking around the place now, we're clearly surrounded by Mayak. I spot a couple of Touched with a powerful signature that reminds me of Chai. None of them are in groups larger than two, though, in keeping with the agreement between Touched and Mayak. The Touched don't gather in large groups, and the Mayak leave them alone. From what I understand, Touched and Mayak fought a kind of very covert war for a time before they came to this agreement.

"Why would they open a bar in Mundane reality?" I ask Chai.

"Because we can," a woman answers.

I turn back towards the bar, swivelling on my bar stool, to find that the bartender is standing just behind us, leaning both arms on the other side of the counter. She looks like an adult, Asian version of Natalie Portman in *Leon*. Sharp black bob, black velvet choker with a silver cross, stripy top. She's also wearing circular sunglasses. Indoors. At night.

My opinion doesn't change just because she's Mayak. Tosser.

I also don't need to try to see past her glamour to detect that she's a predator. It oozes from her. The little hairs on my arms stand to attention, and my heart beats a little faster, no doubt my body's natural reaction at realising on some primal level that it could easily become prey.

"You can't be hunting here," I tell her quickly, voice low. Things are tense enough between Mayak and Mundanes at the moment – the last thing we need is some out-of-control Mayak turning the bar into a bloodbath. And given the magic I can sense leaking from her, she doesn't have much control.

In fact, none of the Mayak here do. They feel young, inexperienced. A number of them look drunk, laughing loudly, their gestures over the top. And all of them leak magic.

Older Mayak, like Mr Sangong and Sarroch, are so restrained with their magic when out in public, I sometimes have a hard time picking up on it even when I'm actively trying to.

"We're not here to hunt," the girl replies, taking off her sunglasses to reveal gleaming black eyes. "Yet."

I frown. "I'm not picking up much in the way of Mundanes here."

The girl pouts. "Yes, I don't know why they're not coming. We had a big launch that was covered in all the right magazines and blogs, but since then, nothing. It's so funny watching Mundanes. They're like chickens, aren't they? So stupid, so ignorant, and so insignificant, and yet they run around, peck, peck, pecking, like what they do actually matters."

"If that's how you spoke to them, no wonder they didn't come back," I reply coldly.

She glares at me. "Of course I didn't speak to them like that. I'm not an idiot. We hired a PR agency and everything — I really don't get why they're not coming."

"They can probably pick up on your magic," Chai says carelessly. "The human subconscious is a powerful thing, and it'll tell them that coming here makes them prey, so they'll feel uncomfortable and stay away."

The girl leans languorously against the counter, cocking her head to the side. "Well, they *are* prey."

I narrow my eyes at her. "And the Mayak Elders have given permission for this bar?"

She waves my question away. "I don't need permission."

"Because Daddy is powerful," Chai replies.

"It's Mummy, actually. We're a matriarchal family."

Chai turns to me and raises an eyebrow. "Huh. Definitely fit for one of my essays."

"Do your essays cover spoilt brats?" I reply. "Because it seems like they're just as common among the Mayak as among humans."

The girl gives us a smile that's more a baring of her teeth. "Careful. If there's no entertainment to be had, maybe we'll have to find some by playing with a Touched." She reaches up to toy with a lock of her hair. "Have you ever had the breath stolen from you?"

The cocktail shaker in front of her reshapes itself so that a long, sharp spike appears from the top of it. "Have you ever had your throat slit by a cocktail shaker?" Chai replies casually.

The girl laughs. "You think that would kill me?"

"No. It would hurt, and more importantly, it would cause a massive scene. And trust me that even if you've managed to get this far without asking for permission, the Mayak Elders will come down on you like several tons of bronze if you attack a Touched in public without just cause, break our agreement, *and* on top of it all cause a scene the humans will hear about. The fact that humans would never come here again would be the least of your worries. The consequences if you reveal the existence of predatory Mayak to humans..."

She curls her lip at him. "I could steal your breath before you could slice my neck."

"Nice try, but you're underestimating my speed. I could slice your neck before you completed stealing my breath, and even once you've stolen it, I can remain conscious without breathing for long enough to do some serious damage. Probably slice you up into pretty ribbons. We humans are remarkably resilient, especially those of us who are Touched by magic." All the delicate little leaves of the copper sculpture start to rearrange themselves into sharp blades that point towards the girl. I'm sure if I look around the bar, I'll find that all nearby metal is suddenly very aggressively pointed towards her.

For a moment she and Chai stare at each other, the tension thrumming in the air between them.

And then the girl rolls her eyes. "I'm not going to stand off with you. I have better things to do with my time."

"Ha." I only just manage not to laugh. She doesn't want to admit that she faced up to Chai and lost. Chai's badass like that.

The girl narrows her eyes at me. "Since you're human, *you* make the humans come to my bar."

My phone rings. It's my father. My mother's out of town, so the fact that he's calling me either means there's a crisis of tsunami-about-to-wipe-out-England proportions, or it's a pocket dial. "As delightful as this conversation is. I have to take this."

I hop down from my bar stool, my motorbike leathers squeaking against the vinyl of the seat.

"What about my humans?" the girl complains.

"Sorry, princess," Chai replies. He throws down some money and his business card. "But if you ever want some proper art to decorate your bar, give me a call."

"Quite the sales pitch," I tell him as we reach the door.

"Oh, don't worry. She's going to call me."

I pick up the phone. "Dad? Are you okay?"

2

I have to stick a finger in my ear to hear my dad as I hurry across the bar to the exit. He's excited and talking so fast I'm having trouble understanding him.

At least one thing is clear—this isn't an SOS because he's cut himself trying to open a tin, or because he's locked himself out of the house and can't remember where we hide the spare key.

Yes, both these things have happened when my mother has been gone in the past. It's a bit like leaving a child alone, really. Mum leaves him pre-cooked meals with the days labelled on each Tupperware, and she calls him to remind him to microwave and eat them.

I step out into the night, and my eyes widen as I finally understand what Dad's telling me.

"Everything okay?" Chai asks me, looking concerned. I nod and lift a finger to ask him to wait.

"You need to take a photo of it, Dad," I tell my father. "Once we hang up, you need to look up at the top of the phone screen for the camera app. No, not an actual camera. The app—application. Yes. It has a little camera lens on it."

It takes a while, but we finally hang up.

The coolness found earlier in the year once the sun goes down is nowhere to be seen now. Instead, the humidity is creeping up so that my riding leathers are already too hot and itchy. This time of year, riding a motorbike is pleasant so long as the motorbike is moving. Walking around in all the gear is a bit of a sweaty trial.

"So what was that about?" Chai asks.

"Dad found something about Qinglong that might relate to me."

Qinglong's the Azure Dragon of the East, one of the Four Guardians of the skies. For some reason I felt a really strong pull to a gate dedicated to her, and then of course there was the massive wave that saved Ari and me—water is Qinglong's element.

My phone chimes softly. It's incredible what powerful motivation can do as far as teaching my father to use technology. If mythology and folklore are on the line, he can actually figure out how to send me a picture.

I open it, heart pounding as I show Chai. "Dad came across a passage in one of his books. He's been looking into Qinglong for me, and Gerabang gate as well, to try to establish what the hell happened there and what my connection to it might be. And look what he found."

The passage reads 'for Qinglong contains within her the essence of all beneath the sky. She is the embodiment of qi or chi, the vital force that imbues both living and inanimate objects.'

"Doesn't that sound like a link to my magic?" I ask. "In a way, what I do is connect to the essence of objects and living creatures, right? I've never thought of it in terms of qi, but I guess I must be doing something like connecting to the qi of things."

Chai nods thoughtfully. "That does sound about right."

"Sarroch made it clear that Qinglong is far too important to come down to our world and have a physical body. That if she left the Eastern skies, magic and the world would fall into chaos. But then again, both Mr Sangong and Ilmu have been somehow sworn to secrecy through the use of magic. Some kind of spell preventing them from telling me the truth about who I am and where I come from. It would take someone powerful to do that, and someone with serious motivation to bother with hiding the origins of a Touched. What if that's why? What if I have a link to Qinglong and for some reason they have to keep that hidden? I'm not trying to be arrogant or deluded in claiming that I have a connection to one of the Four Guardians of the ancient astrology—"

"You're not being arrogant at all. I agree with you. Between the gate, the wave... Qinglong's element is water, isn't it?"

I nod.

"If you have some kind of link to the Azure Dragon of the East, that would make you a pretty damn powerful Touched," Chai says, grinning.

"Let's not get our hopes up. We've all seen first hand that tattoos were useless at improving my magic. And to be honest, I don't care about being powerful. What I do care about is finding out where I've come from."

"Your best bet is going to be Sarroch, then," Chai says. "He might be able to shed some light on all this, unless he's also been sworn to secrecy."

"I don't think so because he's the one who took me to Meng Po, where I found out that I'm an incarnated soul, whatever that means. He doesn't seem to have any problems talking to me about who or what I might be." I quickly scroll through the contacts on my phone. Sarroch picks up after just two rings. "I need to talk to you—it's about the wave from when Ari and I were kidnapped."

"What have you found?"

"I'll tell you when I see you. Where are you?"

"I'm at the Crane."

"Chai and I will be over in about thirty minutes."

"Hold on. Maybe I should come to you."

"Fine. We're at the Scarlet Lounge."

Sarroch scoffs in annoyance. "For crying out loud, Apiya, what are you doing there?"

"What's wrong with the Scarlet Lounge? It's a new bar in town."

"You know very well it's more than that. Mayak younglings are far too volatile for you to be safe around them. You shouldn't be there."

"I have Chai with me," I remind him. "Anyway, if you'd rather we come to the Crane, we can do that. But please make sure Chai can enter as well."

I hang up and look over at Chai. "Sarroch wasn't best pleased that we're at the Scarlet Lounge."

"I doubt he cares about me, pudding. But he's right—you shouldn't come back here on your own."

I sigh. "You know, if I somehow have a connection with Qinglong, you and Sarroch are going to have to stop fussing over me like two mother hens. I've made it this far, haven't I?"

Chai raises an eyebrow at me as he heads over to his car. "How many times have you nearly died?"

I reach my motorbike. "Details," I mutter, unlocking my helmet. A thought occurs to me as I'm about to put it on, and I lower it. "If you knew that this is a Mayak place, does that mean you're trying to get Mayak to buy your sculptures?"

"You've got it in one."

"Why would you bother with that headache? You make plenty of money from humans."

"It's not for the money, but for the challenge. I'd have to be amazing for a Mayak to buy a metal sculpture from a Touched, when so many of them have far stronger abilities with metal than me. But art isn't about strength and power, but about details, balance, composition—it's art, in short. And I'd need to create pieces that speak to them so strongly they're willing to overlook the fact that I'm a Touched."

"And working on spoilt Mayak brats will help with that?"

"Of course. If a spoilt brat wants one of my sculptures, their parents aren't going to say no. Then that's my foot in the door. And of course I also want to get to the Chinese trust fund babies. I've got many fingers, sweetpea, and they're looking for pies to go stick in."

I have to admire his courage and optimism. From where I'm standing, it looks like a massive headache best left alone. "You're making your life difficult for the sake of it."

"For the challenge of it." Chai grins and unlocks his car. "You don't want to hop in with me?"

"It's too nice a night to pass up on a ride. I'll see you there."

* * *

CHAI AND I PULL UP OUTSIDE THE DERELICT BUILDING THAT houses the entrance to the Crane. Wait, let me rephrase that. I pull up outside the building like a normal person would. You know, slow down first and *then* turn to park.

Chai, meanwhile, arrives so fast you'd think he was

fleeing something. He looks like he's going to pass the building, but at the last minute he swerves his car hard and screeches it to a halt so that it's perfectly parked.

I feel for his handbrake.

I'm not a slow rider, not by any stretch of the imagination, but next to Chai I move at a glacial pace. I don't know how much of his incredible driving skills come from human talent and how much from his abilities with metal.

"Auditioning for a stunt driver role?" I ask him as he climbs out.

He laughs, delighted, throwing his keys up in the air and catching them. "I could, you know. Although it'd be tragic to keep my face hidden behind a helmet or a darkened windscreen. The camera loves me."

I swear, anyone else making that kind of statement would sound like a total ass, but Chai can get away with it. It's not just because he truly *is* that good looking and always elegantly put together (tonight he's got on suede loafers, slim cut black trousers, and a tight white long-sleeved shirt that highlights his lean strength). He's just so charming, he can somehow both make it clear that he both means what he says while at the same time poking fun at himself.

I put the bike on its centre stand and chain up my helmet. The heat and humidity immediately begins its assault. I shrug out of my leather jacket. Beneath I only have a grey, cropped t-shirt, but I still have leather trousers and heavy boots to contend with.

The abandoned building in front of us is a perfect illusion. Derelict, dark... The only thing that gives any hint that there's more to it than meets the eye is the enormous decorative bat that hangs upside down at the top of the building, wings spread out wide, a gold ring in its mouth.

Beyond, the night is heavy with the trilling of insects

revelling in the warm and humid temperatures. I shiver as I look over the dark forest that covers the hills stretching up beyond the Crane. That's where Yue stalked me when she was trying to get her hands on the pari-pari egg. The sight of the forest brings back with it the bitter tang of that night's terror.

I shake it off. Yue's not a problem I have to worry about for now.

Chai and I reach the doors, and two guardians materialise on their surfaces. At first they look like paintings until they slowly push themselves out from the wood and become three-dimensional, towering creatures before us.

There's nothing warm or welcoming about them, from their black, articulated and spiked armour, to the large ceremonial weapons they both hold. Their moustaches and chin beards reach all the way down to their chests.

One of them extends a hand mutely towards me, his nails sharp and curved like talons.

"Sarroch is expecting me. Apiya Chapman."

The guardian doesn't so much as twitch a muscle, his blank expression weirdly threatening.

"Sarroch should have left word for me and my guest to be allowed in," I try again.

"Just give the man your hand," Chai whispers.

I reluctantly extend my hand. I hate giving my magical signature. It's the thing that operates as ID in the world of the Mayak. Appearances and names can be changed as easily as clothing for them, but a magical signature cannot be altered.

The thing is, to me, it feels very awkwardly and weirdly intimate, like getting naked and inviting them to have a good, long look.

The guardian's hand is rough and calloused, his sharp

nails digging into the back of my wrist. I can feel him drawing in my magical signature, and I repress a shudder.

As soon as he nods, I snatch my hand away.

Sarroch obviously left instructions for Chai as well because the Guardians don't stop him as he steps across the threshold with me.

The Crane is a world apart from the Scarlet Lounge. Nineteen twenties classic versus twenty-first century poser. Old versus new money. Effortless elegance versus trying too hard.

And the feeling of power here is nothing like the sloppy, leaky magic of the Scarlet Lounge. Back at the Lounge, it was too much—the air was sickly with it. Here, the magic on the air feels heady, ready to turn my head if I'm not careful. The one similarity is the licking-a-battery feel that buzzes all over my skin.

And you have to give it to the older Mayak, they sure know how to dress well. Glittering, beaded flapper dresses. Fine silk cheongsams. Beautifully cut double-breasted suits with brass buttons and heavy pinstripes.

This isn't the timeless finery I've seen them wear at the Grand Mustering I attended. Rather, it's stylish cocktail-wear of another era.

"Well, we've already drawn some attention," Chai murmurs in my ear. Glancing around, I can see what he means. A number of heads have turned to look at us. They aren't outright hostile, but they aren't exactly friendly, either.

Chai stares down the people looking at us and one by one they turn away.

"You glower well," I tell him.

"Well, thank you — I practice in front of the mirror." His tone is light, but I can tell from the tightness in his eyes that he's on high alert.

As fine a place as the Crane is, we're still in a nest of vipers surrounded by a lot of predators who wouldn't think twice about killing us if it suited them. Not all Mayak are predators, but enough of them are to be a cause for concern.

The place is a little different from when I was here last. Thin curtains made of trailing golden chains hang from the ceiling, partitioning the room in small, private nooks. The light shimmers on the chains, making them glitter.

The music is different, too. The voice singing doesn't sound human — in fact, I'm not sure you could even call it singing. It's more like an oddly musical kind of breathing.

The black glass walls remain the same as before, with the brass geometric patterns overlaid on top of them. I can make out the coiling of the smoke-like being inside the glass.

"Do you know what that smoke being is?" I ask Chai, pointing discreetly as the creature ripples through a panel of glass.

He shakes his head. "I'm not sure. What I do know is that it's like a void. Given half a chance it will consume, and consume, and consume."

I remember seeing a woman touching her fingers to the glass, once, and it caused her to bleed, which made her angry. She'd reproached the smoke for taking too much.

We make our way through the crowd slowly. The silk

paintings of cranes hanging on the right wall that give the establishment its name are infused with magic, the cranes gracefully turning their heads to watch us go past.

We're about halfway into the room when I finally make out the stage where the music is coming from. A white sheet has been stretched across it with light shining behind it as if for a shadow puppet show.

Instead, though, something is moving behind the sheet — something that actually looks a bit like thick smoke. Every movement causes an odd, halting, musical breath to escape. The result is odd and yet hauntingly beautiful.

The experience, however, is soured when four mandurugo approach us. The same four Chai fought against, back when I was protecting the pari-pari egg. The same four who tried to kill me for it.

This is a reunion that I could do without.

"We're here as guests of Sarroch," I tell them coldly. "So bugger off."

"Could be we don't feel like it," the mandurugo with the slicked back hair says.

"I get that you're wearing the same clothes as the last time we spoke," I reply, "But that doesn't mean we need to re-enact everything else that happened."

Chai raises an eyebrow. "If I remember correctly, last time my car taught you quite the lesson. Do you want to repeat the experience?"

The chain curtain nearest us begins to sway as if moved by wind, even though there isn't so much as a breeze.

"Or just let us pass so we can find Sarroch," I say tiredly. "And we can avoid a lot of fuss and a lot of mess."

"Ah, but last time we were on our own, and out in the Mundane side of things," Slicked Back replies. "Where we couldn't afford to make a lot of noise. Here, if you start to make a mess, as you put it, I'm sure there will be others who will get involved. Others who are very unlikely to side with you."

I hear Chai take a sharp intake of breath — the chain curtain has suddenly frozen, trembling as if two forces are fighting against each other to move it. Someone else with metal abilities is blocking Chai.

Shit. I glance around.

"I believe my name was mentioned." I turn at the sound of Sarroch's voice. "And yet you did not defer." He's speaking so softly he can barely be heard above the music, and yet there is a deathly chill to his voice. "Guests of mine should not have to make threats to protect themselves."

The four mandurugo pale and take a step back. "We didn't mean... We were just trifling—"

Sarroch snakes a hand out, catching Slicked Back by the throat. His eyes have grown pale as ice, his lips pulling back to bare his teeth. The mandurugo makes a strangled sound and I hear the crunch of bones. "You do not trifle with what is *mine.*"

Sarroch shoves Slicked Back away. His head flops back, boneless, but the other three catch him. I'm not sure whether that's enough to kill him. Probably not.

Sarroch clears his throat and straightens his grey waist-coat. When he looks back at Chai and I, he looks perfectly composed. Nothing would betray that he is anything other than a wealthy businessman in a beautifully cut pair of trousers and waistcoat. That is, other than the wide berth everyone is now giving us.

"This way." He gestures with a hand, politely standing back to let us go ahead of him.

Chai and I exchange a quick look before we walk in the direction Sarroch indicates.

4

We step out of the main room, and into the corridor that leads to the private rooms.

"Seriously?" Chai says, turning back to face Sarroch. "A display of ownership? I do not care to be labelled as yours."

Sarroch shrugs. "It's either that or get attacked by the mandurugo."

"I can defend myself against them."

"Not in the Crane," Sarroch replies flatly.

"I get that you probably don't want fighting in your establishment," I say, "But—"

"The Crane doesn't belong to me," Sarroch replies, frowning.

I'm taken aback. I was so sure he was the owner.

"Whatever your motives," Chai says, "I've worked too hard to establish myself independently to be made a part of 'your' territory in any way. I can look after myself."

"I know you can," Sarroch replies with a sigh. "Had it been anyone else confronting you, I probably wouldn't have felt the need for that display. But those mandurugo are little better than rabid dogs. I don't know what she—" he cuts himself off, pressing his lips into a thin line. "Anyway, that wasn't a proper display of ownership, not in any kind of meaningful way. The mandurugo only respond to a show of force, and that will have done the trick. I haven't officially claimed either of you in the eyes of anyone."

Now, let's be clear, I don't normally care for that alpha-male-she's-my-property kind of thing. Quite the opposite. I know that plenty of human women go nuts for it. Like that TV show—or was it a film?—about American vampires where the vampire's entire dialogue for the movie was reduced to some version of '*she is mine*'.

Yeah, not my thing.

However. There is something uniquely wonderful about a well-muscled man in a waistcoat and white shirt. It highlights the broadness of the shoulders without the crassness of a muscle T-shirt.

Sarroch's shoulders are broad, his chest and stomach hard and flat. And yes, his bum looks great in his great suit trousers—I stole a peek.

So with that in mind, I am prepared to forgive the whole alpha male thing for now. And also sharp cheekbones and anger go well together — who knew?

Plus, he's a weretiger, not a werewolf. Cats don't have alphas—or rather, they all believe themselves as being the ultimate alpha and don't recognise any other as above them. Just ask Tim—he'd tell you that he's Sarroch's superior. I haven't heard of werecats getting into a tizzy over ownership of others the way werewolves do.

"What's so amusing?" Sarroch asks.

I realise I've been smirking to myself. "Oh, nothing."

Chai rolls his eyes at me, having obviously guessed my train of thought.

"I had expected you to be thinking along the same lines as Chai," Sarroch says carefully. "That you'd be annoyed as well." There's a faint question in his tone.

"I have no interest in being anyone's property, but no, I'm not annoyed."

"Oh, right."

I swear I think Sarroch is a little bit pleased. Pleased that I'm not annoyed? That I'm not repulsed by the idea of a little show of ownership on his part?

If that's the case, then colour me happy.

Chai scoffs "Magic help me, will you two stop?"

Sarroch frowns and presses his lips together. He doesn't reply but instead gestures at a half-open door, standing aside.

I glare at Chai as we enter. "Thanks for that," I whisper at him. "Subtle."

"Bad taste in men, Apiya," Chai whispers back. "And appalling timing. Not the time to swoon."

Before I can snap that I wasn't swooning—at least not much—Sarroch enters after us, forcing me to stay silent. I glare at Chai instead.

I was *barely* swooning. It was a swoonette. A micro swoon.

Sarroch is still frowning to himself, as if bothered by something. He clears his throat, looking awkward. "Please rest assured that I'm not in the market to make any acquisitions. At least not permanent ones."

Is that innuendo? Did he just suggest a casual fling, in typical, serious Sarroch way? Because I'd be well up for that. Did I mention the bum looking good in the trousers and the broad shoulders?

"Please take a seat," Sarroch says.

Chai glares at me again. I must have smirked again—

oops. I have no real idea where all this is going, but I'm enjoying finding out.

We're in a new private room, different from the one I've been in before. A collection of colourful Balinese masks hang on a black wall, large, bulbous eyes leering, white teeth and tusks bared.

The rest of the room is black. Gleaming black side tables, black velvet armchairs, black floor. The chrome accents on the furniture stand out starkly.

The room is surprisingly modern, compared to the rest of the place.

"So what did you find out?" Sarroch asks me as he folds himself into a chair with liquid, feline grace.

"Is there anything preventing you from talking to me about who I am or where I come from?" I ask as Chai and I sit down.

"Of course not, why would there be?"

"Both Mr Sangong and Ilmu told me exactly the same phrase when I asked them about the link between me and that wave back at the docks. Same again when I asked about Qinglong, about me being an incarnated soul. As if some kind of spell was preventing them from speaking."

Sarroch leans back in his chair, crossing his legs. He looks thoughtful.

"Is this a common thing?" I ask. "Preventing people from speaking?"

"Only when there is something truly important at stake. And for one to be able to stop Sangong..." He gives me an evaluating look. "Someone extremely powerful must be involved. The question is, why would someone powerful care about the origin of someone Touched by magic?"

"And my father found this," I add, swiping my phone to life and showing him the book passage. "Is it correct?"

Sarroch reads in silence then lowers the phone, looking pensive. "It might be," he said at last. "I'm not completely sure. We don't know as much about the Four Guardians of the skies as we know about each other."

"So the Four Guardians of the skies aren't truly part of the Mayak?" Chai asks. "If they don't have a physical body, they don't come down to our world, and you don't know that much about them..."

"They aren't really, no. Humans and Touched would consider them to be Mayak, but they are both part of us and yet not at the same time."

"If this is correct about Qinglong, that's a potential link to me," I say. "My magic is all about connecting with the qi of things. I hadn't really thought about it that way until now, but now it makes sense."

Sarroch nods slowly.

"Would the Four Guardians be powerful enough to prevent Mr Sangong from speaking?" Chai asks.

"Very much so. The question is, why would they do it?"

"Unless I'm not a Touched." I can't quite work out what the flutter in my stomach is, exactly. Nerves or excitement? "They wouldn't go to the effort of preventing Mr Sangong from speaking of me if I was just a Touched, would they?"

Sarroch shakes his head.

I take a breath. "If I'm not Touched, am I Mayak?"

"No. You don't...feel right. You aren't one of us."

"Then what?"

"I don't know."

"What about your house? The connection I felt to it. Has Qinglong been there in person?"

"No. As I told you, she doesn't come down to our world any more than the other three do."

"Do they watch us?" Chai asks.

"Yes, although I don't know how closely. They guard the skies and keep the balance in the world and in the magic."

"If I have a link to Qinglong, somehow, could she have created the wave back in the docks?" I ask.

Sarroch grimaces and runs a hand through his hair. "I suppose so. But that would be... They aren't supposed to interfere. Interference causes imbalance."

"And we don't want interference, dearest, do we?" a female voice purrs. A voice that I hate hearing.

Yue is standing in the entrance of the room, having opened the door so soundlessly none of us heard her come in. She's wearing an emerald-green silk dress with a plunging neckline. Her black hair ripples and gleams in the soft waves of a forties' movie star. Her lips are red, her eyelids lined with a feline flick of eyeliner.

Yes, in short, she looks as beautiful as she always does. And she clearly knows it. I hate how plain I feel by comparison. Hate that I even think to compare myself to her—I don't normally do that.

She sashays into the room in a rustle of silk.

"What are you doing here?" I ask her coldly.

She turns her head slightly and gives Sarroch a mock coy smile. "I was eavesdropping. So Apiya isn't Touched —interesting."

"Yue..." Sarroch's voice carries a note of warning.

"How you like to worry so." She's reached his chair, and she languidly sits on the armrest and leans across the back so she looks like she's almost draping on him. Then she looks over at me. "He wasn't fully honest, before, when he said he's not the owner of the Crane."

"Yue," Sarroch snaps.

"I am," Yue continues, ignoring him. She gives me a

smile, her white teeth gleaming hard against her blood red lipstick.

I'm a little surprised, although not shocked. I suppose that explains the mandurugo's confidence earlier, since they work for her.

"But since Sarroch is my husband," Yue continues, "The Crane is also his, in a way."

Whoa. It's like a bomb just went off. Forget shock—I've just been gut-punched.

Yue and Sarroch are married? What the hell?

Sarroch looks annoyed, and he jerks his head away when she tries to run the back of her perfectly manicured hand against his cheek. "Stop it, Yue."

Yue freezes for a moment, and then she smiles brightly, as if she doesn't care, but it doesn't come out quite right.

I'm still focused on the bomb that keeps going off in my head. Sarroch is married. To Yue. Who is beautiful and deadly and all the things I am not. This is like a poisoned gift that keeps on giving.

Was I really moments ago wondering if Sarroch was hinting at a fling with me? Jesus, I am next-level delusional. If you'll excuse me, I'm going to get the earth to open up and swallow me whole.

But of course, my magic is far too weak to achieve that.

This is a new record for me. I mean, I know I have poor taste in men, but normally things blow up in my face *after* the liaison has begun, not before.

The worst part of it is that seeing them both together like this, they look right together. Both beautiful, both elegant, both powerful and magical. Next to that, I feel about as attractive as a beetle grub.

And whatever I thought was between Sarroch and I, was

clearly a figment of my imagination. Yes, definitely next-level delusional.

"Api?" Chai asks, and I realise I've been silent for too long. I need to pull myself together.

"I think it would be best," Sarroch begins, and then he freezes, as if listening to something.

Yue pushes herself off the chair as if she too is listening. Then she smiles slowly. "A Great Mustering." She waves her fingers at me. "I'd best be off. Always a delight, Apiya."

She slithers off Sarroch's chair and walks out.

Sarroch rubs his face. He looks tired all of a sudden.

I clear my throat. "Well, I think we'd best get going." So I can go die of mortification in the privacy and comfort of my own home.

My phone beeps, and I check it, grateful for the distraction. My eyebrows shoot up to my fringe as I see the name on my screen.

"What is it?" Chai asks.

"A miracle."

Well, not quite, but as close as. It's a text message from Mr Sangong.

The content of the message is rather less miraculous. My presence is required at the Great Mustering. I guess I'll have to postpone dissolving into mortification.

5

"I think it'd be best if Api and I went to the Mustering by ourselves," Chai tells Sarroch as we stand to leave.

Sarroch looks like he might say something and then thinks better of it. "Yes, you're probably right. Although you can't go in. Only Apiya can, since her presence has been requested."

"I'll escort her to the temple all the same," Chai says, coming to my side and taking my elbow.

I let him guide me out of the room.

"Are you okay?" he whispers to me.

"You mean other than having had my ego pulverised and feeling like the stupidest person in the world? Totally fine. We'll just have to add delusional to my poor track record with men."

"Come on, Api, you couldn't know... And he shouldn't have made allusions to making 'temporary acquisitions', or however he phrased it..."

I don't even feel comforted by the fact that Chai also read that as awkward innuendo.

We reach the main room and fall silent. Numerous

Mayak walk past us, hurrying towards the exit. Some of the Mayak are exiting the Crane as we are, through the doors, although quite a lot are simply winking out—teleporting or something of the sort.

Outside, some of the Mayak are speeding away through the forest, moving with preternatural speed. A few are taking to the skies. And far more prosaically, a glut of cars have suddenly appeared in the car park that was deserted when Chai and I arrived.

"Want me to drive you?" Chai asks.

"No thanks. I *really* need the ride to clear my head, especially if I'm to attend a Mustering."

He nods. "I'll follow by car." I head to my bike, but he stops me with a touch to the arm. "You had no way of knowing he was married, petal. You did nothing wrong. Don't be hard on yourself. If anything, the fault is his for not making that clear from the get go."

"You might be right, but he's not just married to anyone, is he? I know where I stand on the attractiveness scale, and while I don't undersell myself, I don't look like Yue, either. And then there's the fact that he's married to someone so cruel, someone who tried to kill me twice..." I shake my head. "The whole thing is just humiliating, no matter which way you look at it. But don't worry—humiliation never killed anyone. I'll get over it, and who knows? This might be the one that finally teaches me to select more appropriate men to be attracted to."

Chai quirks a smile. "Chance would be a fine thing."

"Ha. Yeah. I'll probably find some other inappropriate one to fall for. At least it's not like I was in love with him or anything, so my feelings aren't hurt, really. Just my pride."

"Well, look at it this way, darling, you *are* making

progress. At least this one didn't have a coke habit and a penchant for hookers."

I snort. "Yep, but at least the cokehead returned my feelings." As evidenced by the barrage of calls and messages he sent after I left him. "This time I made up a whole flirtation in my head. Not sure it's that much better. But thanks for trying to cheer me up."

Chai winks at me. "When this is done I'll be on hand ready to ply you with cocktails."

It's a testament to how crappy I feel that I don't even shudder at the thought of Chai's homemade cocktails. In fact, I positively welcome the idea of them. Nothing short of getting utterly rat-arsed will do tonight, so I might as well do it on Chai's cocktails. "Thanks, Chai. You're the best." I give him a quick hug and then get ready to ride.

* * *

WE REACH LUYANG TEMPLE. WE'RE THE ONLY ONES PARKING our vehicles—Chai does so far more inconspicuously this time. There might have been a stream of people exiting the Crane, but now that we're at the temple, there's no one in sight. The Mayak obviously have more discrete ways of entering. Chai and I are alone, save for the figure standing by the temple's gate.

Mr Sangong.

In the night, as little more than a silhouette, he feels more imposing than the unassuming glamour he normally uses. This is one of the very rare times I can actually sense the power rolling off him. And it's pretty impressive.

Make that seriously impressive.

"Thank you for coming." He comes towards us, walking out of the shadows.

As he steps out of the shadows, the sense of power abruptly disappears, replaced instead by an average sixty-year-old Panongian man in a cheap suit. It's like a switch got flipped.

Yet again, I wonder just what kind of creature Mr Sangong is.

"Why am I required at this Mustering?" I ask.

"They have figured out how Nerong managed to get a baku working for him. Given your involvement, I thought it important that you be here, so I obtained permission to bring you. Chai, I'm afraid I cannot bring anyone else in."

Chai nods. "I expected as much. I just wanted to escort Api. I'll be here when you come out," he adds to me.

I smile at him. "Thanks."

"What will this mean as far as the negotiations with the Mundanes?" Chai asks Mr Sangong.

Mr Sangong hesitates. "It's too early to tell. Hopefully, it will give us some kind of edge which will help, but I fear I might be overly optimistic."

Negotiations between Mundanes and Mayak haven't been going well. When a select few Mayak came out in the open, it caused a lot of excitement, but things are already starting to sour. The humans want the Mayak to register what kind of beings they are, what kind of abilities they have, and they want to set up some kind of tracking system to know where the Mayak are at all times.

Understandably, those Mayak who are out in the open aren't particularly keen on that. The Mayak representative leading the Mayak side of the negotiations, a garuda called Chakrii, has said that they will only consider doing this if all the amulets allowing access to Mayak spaces are surrendered, and the cemeteries handed over to Mayak control so no more amulets can be made. His argument is that the first thing humans did with these amulets was to attempt to kidnap and sell a Mayak to the Chinese, so they clearly cannot be trusted with such powerful a tool.

The Mundanes, however, are refusing to do that, because the amulets represent the only form of defence they have against the Mayak. So neither side is budging, and round and round the talks go.

Meanwhile, people are growing agitated and worried.

A couple of protest groups have sprung up. One of them has named themselves Nature Against Mayak, or NAM, and they decry the Mayak as monsters that have to be controlled. The biggest fuel to their fire is the wave that set Ari and I free, the one that the Mayak have taken responsibility for. A whole slew of natural disasters and other catastrophes are being placed at the Mayak's doorstep. There are enough powerful Mayak in control of natural elements that it could be true, but I know for a fact that it's not.

Unfortunately, the NAM argument is that if the Mayak caused one tsunami wave, they probably caused a lot of other natural disasters. It's compelling for people who don't know different, and it's spreading fear of the Mayak.

On the other side of the arguments are a bunch of religious nutcases who seem to think that this is some kind of judgement day. That the Mayak are here to weigh the quality of everyone's spirit to determine how they will reincarnate. They make signs and give speeches that are nothing short of unhinged. They're pretty harmless, but they help reinforce the impression that the Mayak are neither stable nor good for human society.

In short, there's quite a lot of fuss and little progress. At least the fuss is, so far, confined to rhetoric. But there's enough kindling that if the wrong match is struck, the whole thing could easily go up in flames.

"What about the Scarlet Lounge?" I ask Mr Sangong. "How does that fit into everything?"

He frowns deeply, which for him expresses serious disapproval. "Foolish younglings defying their elders. That is a disaster waiting to happen, but no one is quite sure how to contain it because our young are threatening to cause a scene if we interfere. We cannot afford to draw human attention to them, so for now we have to let them do as they please." Mr Sangong shakes his head. "Utter foolishness. But one thing at a time. For now, let's make it to the Great Mustering. Are you ready to go in?"

I nod.

"I'll be right here," Chai tells me, repeating his earlier assurances. "You call me if there's any trouble."

I promise to do that, even though I know mobile phones don't work within the temple. No point in worrying Chai. I'll be fine with Mr Sangong, anyway.

I think.

6

_____

Mr Sangong and I enter the temple. As we cross the threshold and slip out of Mundane reality and into the Mayak world, I feel the little hairs on my forearms stand up to attention. And then we're through.

All around us is a crowd of Mayak who have clearly only just arrived, everyone heading for their places. I have no idea how they enter—my way is obviously reserved for humans.

The temple is huge, far larger than the equivalent in Mundane reality. The roof is supported by large black pillars covered in gold symbols that don't match anything I've ever seen in the Mundane world. Part of me wishes I could take a photo of them to show my dad, but now isn't the time to look like a tourist. I don't need to call attention to the fact that, by rights, I shouldn't be here.

And in any case, I have no idea if my phone's camera will work here. This space is old — possibly the oldest Mayak space in Panong. I'm not sure. It was built long before modern technology, and therefore allowances for things like mobile signal and Internet weren't made at the time.

Large coils of incense hang overhead, releasing their deep, spicy fragrance. The ember doesn't travel up the incense, instead smoking perpetually so no ash ever crumbles from it. Red silk-tasselled lanterns hang from each pillar, casting a warm glow.

Mr Sangong and I remove our shoes, leaving them among the tidy rows of footwear left behind by the other Mayak. As Mr Sangong leads the way forward, I can feel the warmth of the stone floor through my socks.

Something overhead tugs at my attention—an urge to look up at the ceiling, but I resist it. Last time I came here I saw a huge creature up there, beyond the lanterns and the coils of incense. Something fat and undulating, like a worm, and I have no interest in looking at it again in case it has hypnotic abilities.

The tugging briefly intensifies, like a child pulling insistently at her mother's sleeve, and then it falls away abruptly.

We reach the front of the temple. Ari is already there, dressed casually, in jeans. He smiles at me and says hello discretely.

A quick glance around confirms that a number of other Mayak are dressed in similar fashion — no one was prepared for the gathering, and it seems only those who were at the Crane were already in any kind of formalwear.

I let my eyes slide over Sarroch, as if nothing happened earlier. Pretending to ignore him would be childish and would only highlight my earlier humiliation. Better to look nonchalant.

I really hope Yue isn't nearby.

My nonchalance becomes harder to maintain when Mr Sangong brings us to stand next to Sarroch and Ari. I manoeuvre myself so that Mr Sangong is between us, and then continue to look around, to give myself something to do.

I spot, much to my surprise, Ilmu in her human glamour. She's standing at the edge of a little group of men and women who are apart from the crowd. All of them have a similar, geeky demeanour. The man nearest to her is lanky, hunching forward, blinking nervously from behind thick glasses.

Are they all baku?

Ilmu has been banished, which I had assumed meant she wasn't allowed in these gatherings, but maybe things have changed.

I try for a discreet wave, but Ilmu isn't looking at me, staring straight ahead, face set in a carefully blank expression.

Last time I came here Mucalinda, the enormous seven-headed serpent-like creature, was presiding from atop a low platform. This time, the platform is empty, save for a fat, silk-covered cushion.

And then a hush falls across the crowd. A large man with blue skin enters from the side, stepping out of the darkness to walk towards the platform. Numerous anklets with tiny bells jangle from his ankles, while thick gold bangles gleam at his wrists and biceps.

His chest is bare and gold chains slither across his impressive pectoral muscles. Yet more gold adorns his hair, which flows over his shoulders and down his back in a gleaming black cascade. His eyes are so thickly lashed that the lashes cast a shadow across his cheekbones as he blinks slowly. He wears nothing but a simple, loose skirt wrapped around his hips.

I sense Mr Sangong tensing beside me.

"Shiva," Sarroch murmurs.

"It's his turn," Mr Sangong whispers.

Shiva? The Indian god frequently referred to as The Destroyer? I catch myself—there's no such thing as deities, Indian or otherwise. They are all Mayak. I don't know Indian mythology that well, but I do know that they believe Shiva destroys the old to make space for the new. I'm not sure what the 'old' would be here, but Mr Sangong's reaction doesn't bode well.

Shiva steps up onto the platform and faces the crowd. He looks over us all for a moment and there's a regal tilt to his head as he gazes left and right. Then he slowly sits himself down so that he's cross-legged on the cushion.

And then he lifts a hand and makes a gesture which seems to release a collectively held breath.

The little group Ilmu was on the edge of has re-arranged itself into a row facing the crowd—Ilmu at the edge of it, looking like a bit of a hanger-on. A woman is at the other end of it, and she steps forward. She looks like she might be in her sixties, and she's dressed like a librarian.

"The baku have worked with Akiho, to try to establish what happened to result in him working with a Mundane." Her voice is surprisingly loud and confident given her shy demeanour and body language. "Between his instability and the effect of the kitsune magic, it was extremely difficult to get coherent information from him. We have managed to salvage as much of his memories as we could before he was put to rest."

I feel a small shiver going down my spine. I've heard Ilmu and others say enough times than an unstable baku is a very dangerous thing, so it's probably a good thing that they killed him. But all the same...

"And do those memories cover the period during which

he was working with a Mundane, when he helped kidnap one of our own?" Shiva asks, his voice silky and cold.

"They did. At least, enough for us to get a good picture of what happened." The librarian's expression turns dark. "And what we discovered is—"

"There's no need to beat around the bush. I will happily clarify and explain everything." Yue steps forward.

How has the damned woman had time to change? I swear, she's unable to do anything without making an entrance. She's now wearing a thirties gold lame dress with a plunging neckline and back. The dress glitters in the warm light, her black hair a stark contrast to it and her cream-white skin.

She cocks her head beguilingly as she looks up at Shiva, who smiles fondly back at her. Mucalinda was scary, but at least she didn't seem to buy Yue's crap. Shiva, however, is clearly another kettle of fish. I don't know if a being as powerful as Shiva can be wrapped around someone's finger, but if he can, it probably is Yue's finger.

"Yue," Shiva says warmly. "You will cut to the chase for us?"

Yue gives a teasing smile. "Don't I always?" She turns to face the crowd. "I was the one who put the Mundane and Akiho in contact."

My breath catches in my throat as a roar of voices rises up from the crowd. She did what?

7

"**W**hat would possess you to do such a thing?" Ari explodes. His voice is almost drowned out by all the others shouting.

"Simmer down," Shiva booms. "Allow Yue to explain herself fully. I, for one, am sure she had reasons for doing what she did. We all know that Yue is fiercely loyal to her kind."

Yeah, right. So loyal that she tried to corrupt a pari-pari egg? I keep that thought to myself—something tells me Shiva won't take well to a human interfering.

The crowd quiets down.

"Thank you, Shiva." Yue comes to stand before the platform to make sure everyone can see her. She's clearly enjoying this. I thought I had plumbed the depths of my dislike for her, but oh look, turns out it can run even deeper.

I'm extremely careful not to look in Sarroch's direction—I don't want to see the expression on his face as he looks at his beautiful wife making a scene.

"You all want to condemn my actions, and I can completely understand that," Yue says. "What I have done will come across as a betrayal, especially when we look at the consequences to one of our dearest members, Ari." She sends him an affectionate look, but Ari only scowls back at her.

Damn right.

"But allow me to explain and *then* cast your judgement. Akiho was already unstable, and I knew it wouldn't be long before he would need to be dealt with. But I saw an opportunity. The Mundane known as Nerong already had his amulets and was already surveying Mr Sangong's barbershop. That much I know, and I was surveying him in turn. Which is a good thing, by the way, since no one else seemed aware of him."

Yue doesn't name Mr Sangong, but she looks at him, the implication of incompetence on his part clear. A very neat way to discredit him without forcing a clumsy and public loss of face on him.

A small crease appears between Mr Sangong's eyebrows.

"I decided to give Nerong access to the baku," Yue continues. "It was only a matter of time before he found out more about us, anyway. By doing this, I gave him access to an enormous amount of knowledge and wisdom, which I thought was the best way to dive straight into the heart of his intentions. If he was merely seeking to deepen his understanding of our kind, if he was seeking answers to questions of life or spirituality, if he was seeking solutions to problems the Mundanes face—in short, if there was anything honourable about him, I had just given him the means to achieve his ends. There was, of course, the risk that Akiho would lose control and devour Nerong's memories, but I felt confident that he would have enough strength to hold on, and I was right. And if I'd been wrong, well, there's little harm in a human losing his memories to a baku."

"Akiho is how Nerong identified me and kidnapped me." Sarroch's voice cracked hard against the stone. "Do you understand that?"

Yue ignores him. "What I did is prove that we cannot afford to give humans our trust or knowledge. The moment we do, they will turn on us at the first opportunity, the way Nerong did. We are discussing the possibilities of peaceful cohabitation with the Mundanes, and we are negotiating with them. But what I have shown you is that there can be no peaceful cohabitation between our kind and theirs. If they can find ways to enslave us, they will. The only reason they haven't so far is because we are able to exert more power and strength than them. The Mundanes only respond to strength. To power. To money. They have no respect. No decency. This dream that Sangong sold us, this idea that we could all one day live peacefully, is just that: a dream. Or rather there can be peace, but only after the Mayak have exerted full power and control over humanity."

Oh, this is bad. Out of the corner of my eye, I see Mr Sangong close his eyes and take a deep breath.

"Tell me I'm wrong," Yue says softly. "What have we seen of the humans so far to make us believe that they can be trusted? First Sarroch, and then Ari. They have had plenty of opportunity to prove themselves worthy of our trust. Worthy of us deigning to come forward to them once more. But humans are nothing more than—"

"My parents." The words blurt themselves out of my mouth before I can consider what I'm doing.

"What?" Yue snaps. She turns to skewer me with a look.

"My parents have known about the Mayak for a long time, now," I say quickly. "And they have always been friends to the Mayak. They kept your secret. They presented at the Crane to help give you all as much information as possible so that you would be able to decide which Mayak should come out to the public first. They have not used the knowledge they have towards any nefarious ends."

As I feel the pressure of thousands of eyes looking at me, it occurs to me that mentioning my parents might have been a mistake. The last thing I want is to have some minion of Yue's showing up at their house.

"I've been hearing about this pet Touched," Shiva says, leaning forward and peering at me like I'm some exotic creature. "Times really *are* changing. Is she yours, Sangong?"

Mr Sangong touches my arm, a subtle invitation for me to step back, and as I do, he steps forward.

"I think we should be cautious not to judge the whole of humanity by the actions of one man," he says, ignoring Shiva's question about me. "After all, when faced with the news that the pari-pari had conceived an egg, Yue didn't help the pari-pari to successfully hatch their youngling, knowing how hard it is these days for them to reproduce. Instead, she went after the egg, attempting to take it for herself so she could pervert it into a weapon."

Mutters run through the room at this reminder. Yue's face darkens.

"Does that mean all of us would do the same if confronted with that choice?" Mr Sangong continues. "Of course not. We are all different, and we have our own minds. Just as not all humans condone Nerong's actions. Apiya was right in mentioning her parents just now. They are nothing like Nerong, and I agree that they have so far been allies to the Mayak. We shouldn't be too hasty in declaring humanity as dangerous. Peace is always the preferable route, and peaceful cohabitation is the best possible outcome for everyone."

Yue's face has grown tight, her eyes angry. She opens her mouth to speak, but Shiva raises a hand to stop her.

"I agree that peaceful cohabitation is the best solution," he booms. I let out a relieved breath. "However, I am of the opinion that such cohabitation will not be possible so long as Mundanes continue to be so numerous. We are in an imbalance, and that needs to be righted first. I myself am in favour of a cull. Not so severe that the magic is impacted. It remains a mystery to even us Elders why magic requires the presence of Mundanes in the world in order to be in balance. But fewer numbers would remove the humans' greatest advantage—their numbers—meaning we can be confident in our abilities to overpower them as and when needed. From such a position of strength, we can then cohabitate with them completely openly."

That's not cohabitation. That's domination.

"Remember how it was, in the past," Shiva continues. "Humanity loved us, worshipped us, and we cared for them. Why, I swallowed poison to save humanity, once."

Ah yes, that's another myth about Shiva, which is clearly true. The myth is supposed to explain why his skin is blue.

"Humanity was small, back then. Fragile. In need of our protection. Which is why I did what I did, to preserve them, and I do not regret it for one instant. If we cull the humans down, they will have no choice but to once again respect and worship us, as they should. It is no coincidence that the rift between our kinds occurred once humans became more numerous."

Yue gives a deep shudder, a slow, ecstatic smile blooming on her face. "So we go to war."

Shiva shakes his head. "Were it only up to me, I would

take my chariot of fire this day and ride out to lead the cull. But not all Elders think as I do, and we must have an agreement, or at least a majority." He raises a hand to stop Yue, who was about to speak. "We are still too divided, so for now there can be no war. We all agreed about some of ours coming out into the open, because those of us in favour of a cull believe they can be used to distract humans the better to plan our attack. Now we have to agree on the next step."

Yue frowns. "And while we deliberate and hesitate, humans attack defenceless Mayak."

"I'm far from defenceless," Ari growls.

"Dearest Ari," she purrs. "You know how highly I think of you, and how fondly..."

If I hadn't already known that Ari and Yue have history, the look in her eye just then would have made it perfectly clear. So clearly, she's not worried about being faithful to her husband. Or letting that be known. Ari looks away.

Or maybe Yue and Sarroch have some kind of arrangement... I don't want to know.

"But the fact remains that Mundanes were able to capture you," Yue continues. "It is not a reflection of your abilities, but of the power and danger they represent. We cannot underestimate the threat they pose to us." She turns to face Shiva once more. "If we are to act, we must act swiftly."

Shiva frowns. "It is unbecoming of a Mayak of your age to caution haste. The Mayak do not hasten. We live eternal and time means nothing to us. We will take action when the time is right, and not before. So I have spoken."

8

I wake up the following morning grumpy and hungover. Chai was as good as his words, and once the Mustering was over he invited me to his place and dutifully plied me with buckets of alcohol while we set the world to rights.

We discussed the situation with the Mayak and the Mundanes at length, of course, and then the fact that Sarroch is married.

The thought makes me groan and bury my face into my pillow. It's not just the fact that he is married. That would be embarrassing, but I could get past it. It's the fact that he is married to *Yue*. That *Yue* is the person he chose out of all others.

Something about that is exquisitely humiliating – what the hell was I thinking, that I might have any kind of shot?

Chai was his usual adorable and brilliant self last night. He got as drunk as me, and by the end of the evening he was making outlandish statements, such as if he were to turn into a straight man he would have eyes only for me.

Bless him.

My phone vibrates, and I pick it up. A message from Sarroch asking if we can meet to talk. Apparently he wants to explain about last night.

I really fail to see what there is to explain. He's married to Yue, end of story. I really hope he's not going to throw some cliché at me, something about him and Yue being estranged, or something like that.

Divorce was invented for a reason.

Much as I'm a disaster on the dating front, my rule about not breaking up relationships is iron clad. I don't care what the situation is, I *only* ever date single men.

Anyway, none of this matters – I really don't want to see him or talk to him right now. But seeing as I'm hungover, I don't feel like having to send an awkward message expressing that sentiment, so I do a very adult thing instead.

I ignore the message. And I don't mean ignore it for now with the intention of replying later. I delete the message and put the phone down. There we go. Sorted.

At some point I will have to see Sarroch again, but that is for future non-hungover-me to deal with.

My phone vibrates again. Is it pathetic that a small part of me hopes it's Sarroch trying again to reach me?

Don't answer that, I know it's pathetic. Blame it on the shrivelled state of my brain.

Thankfully, this time it's a call from my mother. I ignore that, too. She has the most uncanny Mother Radar, and she can always tell when something is wrong, no matter how hard I try to hide it.

She probably has some kind of bat radar allowing her to pick up on the fact that, halfway across the world, her daughter is upset.

Don't get me wrong, it's wonderful that she's so attuned to my emotions and that she cares so much. I'm just grumpy, and I really don't want to answer questions either about the state of the Mundane-Mayak negotiations, or about the disaster that is my imaginary love life. Seriously, how did I think I had a shot with Sarroch?

Before I reach new, previously undiscovered levels of patheticness and self-pity, I get out of bed. There is one thing that is sure to make everything feel okay again.

I throw open the bedroom door to be greeted by a fiercely wagging, plumed tail following thirty kilos of excited golden fur.

Last night was supposed to be my day off from the barbershop, but I'm way more exhausted than if I'd spent the evening working. Good thing I'm back at work tonight – I'm not sure I could handle a second night off in a row.

For now, though, I'm going to spend the day with Hunter and my animals and enjoy a bit of peace and quiet.

* * *

GRANNIES THE WORLD OVER HAVE GOT IT RIGHT. IT IS TRULY wonderful to potter in a garden.

Hunter and I went for a big hike together, and I didn't even mind when he found some wild boar poo and rolled in it. Thoroughly.

Now I'm tinkering in the garden, transferring my pineapple plant from one pot into the other. Forget the possibility of a war between Mundanes and Mayak – I might be able to get fresh pineapple from my own courtyard. Can you imagine how *awesome* that would be?

The afternoon sun is warm on the back of my neck, only just hot on the edges. The soil is cool and moist beneath my fingers. Flying insects buzz about lazily, and the air is fragrant with the perfume of my potted frangipani tree.

There's no other time of year when the temperature is so pleasant at this time of day, when the light filters through the leaves of my miniature palm in just the right way, turning green-tinged gold as it dapples the flagstones beneath.

Paradise.

My two rabbits and my guinea pig are busy chomping down on a veritable feast of carrot and cucumber peels. Barung, the bar-bellied pita bird I rescued (he has a busted wing) has hopped up onto one of the perches I set out for him in the shade, and is currently busy preening his feathers.

Fergie is up to his usual tricks, making a dash for my trellis. It's a tortoise dash, so I have plenty of time before I need to catch him to stop him climbing and wedging himself behind it.

I also check on Frank the frog. He's hiding away in his little rocky haven, a crevice that remains cool and moist in all but the hottest part of summer.

Hunter, meanwhile, is lying down by the pond, which has become his usual spot of late. I crouch down next to him and stroke his ears.

He's looking at the fish we rescued—he's grown quite obsessed with it. The fish has done nothing to suggest it's anything other than a normal fish. Nothing except that it randomly appeared on the grass of a park near the waterfront, of course.

It has royal blue and silver scales with a crest of livid red marks along its back. Its fins are delicately feathered. It has a set of little moustaches which made me think it was a kind of koi carp at first, but while it looks similar, its markings don't match any of the breeds.

I spent a lot of time googling it, and I even took out a

book from the library called Freshwater Fish of Southeast Asia, in an attempt to identify it. To no one's great surprise, my searches came up empty.

"Why is he so interested in a fish?" a voice asks.

"Hi Tim." I don't turn around to greet the cat. He has ways of sneaking in and out of my house, which I have to admit are quite impressive. "He's probably interested in it because it's a magical fish."

"Hmm. It's a pretty boring fish, if you ask me."

"No one asked you. And no one asked you to pay attention to it, either. If you don't like it, go somewhere else."

"Ooh, aren't we grumpy today?"

I don't bother answering that.

Tim stretches and yawns, then he walks in front of me, his tail high. He purposefully makes sure the tip of his tail brushes against the underside of my nose. That, by the way, is a feline way to display condescension.

Honestly, I don't know why anyone chooses to have a cat. The constant stream of patronisation and insults is enough to test even a Buddhist monk's patience. Cat owners must be masochists.

Tim finds a spot in the sun and gets comfortable. I'm not a cat owner, by the way. Tim isn't mine. He has simply chosen to keep coming back to my place, and there's precious little I can do about it.

Which I suppose is how it works for most cat owners. They get chosen by a cat and then have to put up with the cat's attitude.

I turn my attention back to my pineapple plant and settle it in its larger pot, connecting with it and suggesting that it should get comfortable and use the extra space to grow big and strong so it can make me a pineapple. I can sense its willingness twinned with its discomfort at having been moved.

"Sorry, little guy," I tell it. "Had to be done. You outgrew your last pot."

Pineapples thrust straight out of the middle of the plant —did you know that? Like a fist raised in defiance at the sky. I can't wait to see my first pineapple arrive. Speaking of defiance.... I glance over my shoulder.

Fergie is still doggedly heading towards my tomato trellis, and he's getting close, now.

"Not the time to climb, Ferg." I pick him up, his stubby little legs waving slowly and uselessly in protest. "You'll squish my tomatoes. All four of them." I put him down on the other side of the courtyard, next to the rabbit hutch.

Then I sigh with contentment as I turn to weeding. After last night's drama, this little beat of normality and mundane activity is the most soothing thing I could have hoped for.

After a while, I look back over my shoulder to check on Fergie and make sure he's not heading for the trellis again. Defeat does not feature in his DNA. I eventually locate him inside the rabbit hutch.

Given that the hutch is a foot off the ground, that's quite the feat, even for Fergie.

Methinks he had some assistance from Zer, the pari-pari youngling, who's now crouched underneath the hutch. His skin has shifted to be remarkably close to the pine the hutch is made from. He looks up at me mistrustfully. I don't know why, but I've not been able to bond with Zer in any way. He loves my animals and my courtyard, but doesn't seem to want any interaction with me...

I've tried reaching for him with my magic, but it's like facing a wall. I just can't get past it. I was able to connect with him just once, when he hatched out of his egg. But since then...nothing.

Before I can think of something new to try to create a fraction of connection between us, a knock at the door interrupts me.

Hunter stands up at once and barks. I frown. I'm not expecting anyone. I hope Sarroch hasn't dared come to my house.... And yes, if he has, I *will* slam the door in his face.

Hunter has run inside the house and is still barking, clearly agitated. I step into the kitchen and grab an old rag to wipe the soil off my hands. I leave the rag on the kitchen counter and head into the living room, frowning.

As I reach with my magic, I sense a Mayak on the other side of the door. I'm unable to sense much more. Whoever it is, they're obscuring their magical signature. But I'm willing to bet it's Sarroch. He's able to hide his signature, and he's probably doing it in the hope that I'll answer the door.

Ha. Well. He's about to get an earful. When I ignore a message, that's not an invitation to come bother me when I'm in the middle of gardening.

I don't care what he has to say. I'm not interested in explanations—I've had all the explanations I need.

And more to the point, I want space to lick the wounds to my pride, get myself over my stupid crush double quick, so I can go back to normal. And that will *not* be helped if Sarroch shows up at my house. I won't tell him that, of course. I think slamming the door in his face will be plenty.

I open the door.

And find Yue smiling coldly at me.

9

S hock slows my movements, so she pushes in before I have a chance to slam the door in her face.

"You do not have an invitation to enter my house," I say quickly.

She gives me a look. "Please. That stuff only works for vampires. I'm a *pontianak*." She folds the sun umbrella she was using to stop herself from tanning. Heaven forbid her skin be anything less than porcelain-perfect.

She looks around. "I see your house is as underwhelming as the rest of you."

She's wearing a bright red halter-neck fifties dress with a flaring skirt, cream high heels, and of course her makeup and hair look like she's just stepped out of a film.

By contrast my fringe is damp and stuck to my forehead, I probably have soil somewhere on my face, and I'm wearing a t-shirt that reads 'Screw world peace, I want a pony'.

Oh, don't I feel beautiful and classy.

"Yes, my house is unimpressive, and I'm unimpressive, so don't waste any more of your precious time here, and leave."

Something invisible feels like it suddenly has clamped

down around my throat, making it hard to breathe. I recognise the suffocating sensation. Yue has done this to me once before.

Except that last time Sarroch was present, and she clearly only did it to scare me. Hunter's barking turns frenzied. My hands fly to my throat but find nothing to grab.

"Close the door, there's a good girl," Yue says sweetly.

I find myself unable to do anything other than obey. Still gasping for air, I close the door stiffly, my limbs moving of their own accord.

Yue releases me, and I take a deep, shuddering breath.

"What the hell was that for?" I snarl. "Why are you here?"

"I wanted to see where you lived."

"Why the hell would you care about where I live?"

"I wanted to know what people would see when they find your body." Her attack is so rapid, I'm amazed I'm able to get my arms up fast enough to block.

The impact of her arm against mine sends a shock-wave of pain shrieking up my bones. Possible hairline fracture.

With a growl, Hunter throws himself at her. She backhands him away, and he goes flying, landing heavily in a whimper of pain.

"Hunter!" He struggles to get up, his left foreleg obviously broken.

I shouldn't have allowed my attention to move off Yue.

Mistake.

I'm too slow when I try to dodge her next blow. She flings her hand at me lazily, and her talon-like nails catch the side of my neck.

I let out a strangled cry, both hands flying to the wound as I stagger back. I press down even as I feel the blood leaking through my fingers.

I stumble further back towards my kitchen.

Yue cocks her head at me and smiles. She lifts her right hand — her fingers are red with my blood. She licks the blood off her middle finger with obvious relish.

"I find it helps to wear red on occasions such as this." She smiles at me. "I'll finish him off first, while you are still able to watch."

Hunter. I can't even find the strength to shout his name. If I move my hands and release the pressure, I'll bleed out in short order.

"No." The sound is little more than a gurgle. "No." I stumble after her, tears blurring my eyes, blood seeping through my fingers.

Yue stalks over to Hunter, and he whines and whimpers as he desperately tries to scramble away from her. His broken leg is hobbling him.

Hunter. No.

A black ball of fur darts in between the two of them

Tim yells and spits, his ears pinned back against his head.

Yue pauses, frowning. "Get away, little cat. My argument isn't with you."

But Tim continues to growl and hiss. Yue takes a step towards Hunter, and I sense the impact of two energies going up against each other.

Yue stops, looking surprised.

"Hunter," I croak. "Come here." Hunter whimpers and whines, but he hobbles towards me.

I continue back towards the kitchen, drawing Hunter to me and away from Yue.

She's between me and the front door. She is also between me and my phone. It might as well be in Kathmandu for all the chance I'd have of getting to it right now.

Hunter reaches me, and we retreat into the kitchen.

The pressure between Tim and Yue is increasing, and little by little Tim is giving ground. Yue is slowly advancing towards the kitchen.

I smell ozone.

Yue smiles triumphantly.

She'll reach the kitchen soon. There's nothing I can do. Panic makes it hard to breathe. Or maybe it's my wound.

There's nothing I can do. Nothing.

The thought bounces over and over in my head.

And then I hear a sound I've never heard before. Like an angry fox screeching.

Zer is crossing my kitchen, her tiny fists clenched, her face the picture of outrage. She is now most definitely a girl once again, and I've never seen her so angry.

She makes another noise.

Yue pulls back briefly, obviously surprised.

And then vines covered with leaves shoot out of my kitchen walls between us and Yue. They cross the entrance to the living room and twine with each other.

"Stop that," Yue snaps. She reaches for the vines and tears them apart, but more and more burst out of my walls, rapidly weaving a barrier. Tim hops through a gap just before another vine shoots out and fills it. "Stop! I order you to stop!"

I briefly sense a wave of power, a tightening in my throat, but it stops abruptly. Zer shrieks again.

Yue screams in rage and frustration, tearing at the vegetation that only grows more and more thick.

The tiny pari-pari stays as she is, her little face intent as she glares at the vines. More vines are sprouting from the ceilings and the walls, slowly enclosing us in a little vegetation bubble. The bubble doesn't close off the courtyard, instead encasing it, so both courtyard and kitchen are completely cut off from the rest of the world.

And then the noise and the movement on the other side of the vines stops.

"Well, I'll just take your phone with me," Yue says, her voice once again all sweetness. "Without it, you'll just bleed out in your kitchen. A shame I won't get to kill you myself, but the end result will be the same. And at least I'll have the satisfaction of knowing I caused your death."

I hear her footsteps and the sound of my front door opening and closing.

As if obeying her prediction, my legs suddenly buckle and I only just manage to control my fall until I'm sitting on my kitchen floor, leaning against the cabinets. Hunter wines, awkwardly shuffling as best he can with his broken leg, to lie next to me.

"Tea towel," I manage to whisper to Tim.

Tim hops up on the kitchen counter to grab the rag I wiped the soil off my hands with.

No time to think about bacteria. If I lose too much blood, there won't be anything left to infect.

Breathing against the terror of releasing the wound at my neck, I reach out my right hand, snatch the rag, and then stuff it against the wound, pressing both hands against it.

"Tim," I croak, "Get help."

"Back as soon as I can, treacle," he replies quickly.

He pads over to the vines that now block the entrance to the kitchen. They are still coiling around each other, like living things. The foliage is growing thicker and more dense.

Tim hesitates, obviously looking for a way to slip out, then he turns back towards the courtyard. He hovers at the entrance — I'm guessing the vegetation is also too thick here for him to get past.

"Use... Magic," I croak.

"I can't." Tim looks back to look at me. "I can use magic to slip away through human-made walls and doors, and also out of the barbershop because Mr Sangong allows it. But this is different. I... I can't get past it."

I close my eyes. My strength seems to be slowly flowing out of me with the blood that leaks out of my neck. The rag is slowly growing damp beneath my fingers.

"Zer," I whisper. "Let Tim out. Let..."

Zer looks at me and coos, tilting her head and looking worried. She crouches down next to me and places to her pudgy little hand on my thigh.

"Let Tim out." Zer looks at Hunter, and then something like understanding blooms on her face. Thank god. "Yes, let Tim out."

Zer settles herself to lie next to me, just like Hunter is doing. She coos as she curls into a little ball against me.

"No. Let Tim out. I need..." I don't finish the phrase, knowing full well it will be of no use. She doesn't understand Panongian, and I doubt she speaks English, either. "Tim? Can you...speak to her?"

Tim makes a few noises, but Zer doesn't react. She's staring at Hunter across from me. I get the sense that Hunter could tell her what to do, but I have no idea how to communicate that to him.

It's a couple of hours yet before my shift is due to start at the barbershop — and therefore a couple of hours before anyone will notice that I'm missing.

If I stay as I am, I will just bleed out. I feel tears filling my eyes and a low keening sound escapes me — I'm not ready to die.

Tim comes and sits next to me. "I don't know what to do, princess." He sounds genuinely distressed.

"Call... Sangong?"

"I already tried. Whatever magic Zer has, I can't get past any of it. She's completely sealed us off. It'll be why Yue couldn't get to us, but it means we can't get to anyone else."

So I basically have no options but to hope I last long enough to still be alive by the time someone comes looking for me.

Yue has my phone—she'll be able to reply to any messages from Chai, so he's unlikely to worry, not at first. Not fast enough.

My first client is Kamlai, and I never miss an appointment with her. She will notice my absence. If I get lucky, she'll do more than just message my phone.

I just have to hang on long enough. Have to find a way to slow the blood flow...

My blood. If I was able to draw the ketamine out of Ari and into myself, could I draw my own blood back into itself? If not stop, then at least slow the flow from the wound at my neck?

I close my eyes and focus my attention inwards, reaching for my blood. Reaching for the qi of my blood, no longer caring whether that's a thing, whether that's possible.

It's my own body — there is nothing in the world I know better, nothing in the world that knows me better. And my blood's natural way of being is not to be pouring out of me and onto my kitchen floor.

I focus all my attention, all the strength I'm able to summon, and draw my own blood back inside me.

I lose all sense of time and place. I'm vaguely aware of a weight on my legs, and then I feel something warm and fluffy settle on my stomach. More warmth, more fluff on my legs. I recognise the tiny light presence that hops all the way up to my chest. It's my bird, Barung.

The knowledge of all my animals around me gives me a measure of courage and strength. I don't know if I'm actually drawing it from them or if it's just knowing that I'm not alone. I double down on my concentration.

All sense of the outside world disappears as I spiral deeper and deeper within, drawing my own blood, my own energy back into myself.

10

The sound of voices abruptly brings me back to myself. I have no idea how much time has passed. My hands still press the rag against my neck, but it's soaked through, now. And I feel cold, dreadfully cold.

"I'm telling you, Apiya has never missed one of my appointments. Something is wrong, I can feel it."

Kamlai's voice is distant and muffled from beyond my front door.

"She's not replying to her phone, but then she hasn't been replying to me, recently." That's Sarroch.

That tugs my attention away from my blood and I feel a fresh wave of it spilling out of my neck and down my fingers. I scramble to get my attention focused once more.

"We are in here!" Tim yells. "We need help! Apiya's badly injured."

The sound of my door opening. Cursing and rapid footsteps. Tearing at the vegetation that blocks my kitchen entrance.

Zer makes a low growling sound. The vines begin to tighten once more.

"No, Zer. Stop." I release my left hand and reach for her. "Let him in."

That was a mistake. Fresh blood pours out over the fingers I still have over the wound.

Even as I move my left hand back to the wound as quickly as I can, in spite of how cold and leaden it feels, I feel my consciousness spiral away from me.

"No.... No..."

I feel a brief spike of utter terror. I can't die. Not like this. Not now.

An entirely foreign sensation rushes through me. It's as if an enormous being has suddenly blown air throughout my body, pushing my consciousness back to me.

I press on the rag once more, returning my attention to drawing my blood back to me. That's all I can do. Sarroch has to get past Zer's obstacle by himself.

I concentrate my attention on my blood once more, dimly aware that someone or something is tapping a rapid rhythm against a hard surface. And then I realise that my teeth are chattering.

Zer coos at me again.

I feel her reaching for me through her magic. We connect for the first time. Gasping, I reach for her in turn, focusing everything I can into the suggestion that she open up, let the people in.

"Stand back," Kamlai suddenly orders.

Sarroch's scrambling at the vines stops. I keep my eyes closed, keeping my attention focused on both my blood and trying to convince Zer to let them in.

And then I feel Fergie slowly clamber down from the spot on my legs. I crack open an eyelid to see him doggedly heading towards the vines.

Zer allows a tiny crack to open. Kamlai's scaled and

moist front paw slips in, with its blunt claws. She makes a low, wet rumbling noises. Fergie seems absolutely mesmerised, hurrying towards her as fast as his stubby little legs will carry him.

Again Kamlai makes the rumbling noises. Fergie seems to be responding to her somehow.

Maybe it's seeing that Fergie trusts Kamlai, but I sense Zer relax next to me. All at once the vines relax, opening wide.

"Apiya!" Sarroch and Kamlai are at my side at once.

The relief at having help at hand causes me to lose focus completely. Blood once again begins to cascade out of the wound at my neck, but I'm too exhausted to find my focus once more.

Sarroch barks something at Kamlai in a language I don't understand. Kamlai trembles, the shaking growing worse until the floor and walls are also trembling from the strength of her shaking. Something crashes and breaks, as if my house is being rocked by an earthquake.

Sarroch sweeps me up into his arms and takes me to the sofa. I'm distantly aware that I'm making bloodstains on my couch and that it will be a nightmare to remove.

Kamlai stops shaking abruptly. A little old woman has appeared at my front door—the healer who took care of me after I nearly killed myself removing the silver from Sarroch's cage. She's dressed in black as usual, looking like little more than an ancient, wizened old woman.

"Apiya needs your assistance, oh wise one," Kamlai says with a respectful bow of her head.

The healer sucks at her teeth and looks at me with disapproval. Nothing new there.

As she comes to my side I briefly lose time and swim back to consciousness to find her muttering over me. I reach up to my neck, realising I've completely let go. Blood must be pouring out.

The old healer snaps angrily and slaps my hands away. Instead, she pushes something small and hard into the wound that makes me scream with pain.

I struggle ineffectually against her, too weak to actually form words. Sarroch holds me down easily.

Whatever she shoved into the wound quickly stops being round and smooth, instead spreading out tendrils inside my neck.

The pain is like nothing I've endured before. It's like having slivers of bamboo pushing underneath my skin. Like having needles pushing forward all the way into my brain.

Hunter is barking and whining.

My vision grows patchy, my consciousness once again spiralling away from me.

"No! We need to keep her awake."

Something bites my right arm, and a feeling like ice flows into my vein. The shock of it yanks me awake. Kamlai is holding my wrist in her teeth.

"Good," the little healer says. "We've stemmed the blood flow, but now we need to replace what was lost or she won't last very long."

"She'll live?" Sarroch asks roughly.

The healer sucks on her teeth. "She'll live. Not that she deserves to. Foolish girl."

* * *

IT'S HARD TO KNOW HOW MUCH TIME PASSES. WHEN I FALL out of consciousness, Kamlai bites me some more to bring me back. The pain of what the little healer does to me sometimes makes me scream, sometimes makes me black out, before Kamlai brings me back.

But slowly I regain strength, or rather I no longer feel like life is leaking out of me.

"All right, I've done as much as I can do," the healer announces. "Prepare yourself. I'm going to start removing the crawlers."

"The crawlers?" I ask faintly.

The healer nods. "We'll take it slow, one by one."

"One by one? You only put one thing in my neck."

"Indeed. A full colony of them. And given the amount of blood they've been able to glut on, they're unlikely to come willingly, so this might be a bit painful."

The thought of more pain makes me feel nauseous, and I grit my teeth. "Where is Hunter?" Let's not dwell on the thought that I have things crawling in my neck and drinking my blood.

"I'll bring him," Sarroch says.

He steps away, and I hear Hunter growl. He's interrupted by an irritated tiger's roar. Hunter's growl fades to a whimper.

Sarroch returns carrying my dog and gently places him down on the sofa next to me. As soon as I'm able to rest a hand on him, I feel a small degree of strength.

"Okay, do your worst," I tell the healer.

She nods grimly and reaches for the wound at my neck. Whatever it is she tugs on, it's like a whole network of pain lights up, a spiderweb that reaches all the way up to my brain.

Then she rips something away and drops it with a little clink into bowl prepared for that purpose. A tiny creature with a flat body scuttles angrily about the bowl. It's covered in my blood.

The healer bends over my neck and I feel something cool followed by a sharp pain. This time, though, there's something satisfying about the pain because I can feel that something has been closed.

"Next one." The healer extends too long fingernails towards my neck and grabs hold of another of the creatures, sending more pain screaming up into my skull.

11

Finally, the healer is finished. The bowl is full of these tiny crawling creatures, and the thought that they were not long ago running up and down my neck makes me shudder with revulsion.

Sarroch and Kamlai, who has once again donned her human glamour, help me sit upright on the sofa. Hunter shuffles awkwardly forward to rest his head on my lap.

"I'm so relieved you're okay," Kamlai tells me.

"Me too," I reply. "I wasn't quite ready to die yet."

"You won't die today," the healer sniffs. "But one day, I won't be around to help, or I will get there too late. Your body is only human, Apiya. You cannot keep acting as if it's made of magic."

I'd like to argue back that I didn't do anything in this instance. I was bloody *gardening* when I was attacked. How much more inoffensive can I get than gardening? But I'm too exhausted to summon up the energy for an argument.

Later.

"I will be back in a couple of hours," the healer

announces. "Until the blue has been fully absorbed, no sudden or strenuous movements."

"I will stay and look after her," Sarroch replies.

A tiny part of me wants to protest at that, but I'm far too weak and tired to really care who looks after me, so long as I'm safe.

Sarroch escorts the healer and Kamlai out, and since I'm not particularly eager to engage in any kind of conversation with him — and since I'm absolutely exhausted—I'm quite happy to drift off into sleep before they reach the door.

* * *

WHEN I WAKE UP, I FIND MYSELF IN MY BED. I AM — thankfully — still wearing my own clothes, even though my top is crusted with dried blood. I'm just not ready for the very particular embarrassment of having someone change my clothes while I'm passed out.

Especially not Sarroch.

It's nighttime, but someone — probably Sarroch — switched on my bedside table lamp, which casts a warm glow over the room. I breathe in the familiar, safe sight of it. All of my things are just as they should be—neat and tidy, and no sign of what happened downstairs.

Ever the enthusiast, Hunter attempts to get closer to me, but his broken leg hampers him. I'm not sure if the healer tended to it or if Sarroch was able to arrange for a vet, but his leg is, thankfully, splinted and bound.

He whines and whimpers as he shuffles over to lick my face. I smile and stroke his head, although I move oh so carefully, not wanting to risk any strain on my neck.

I wonder if Hunter understands how close I came to dying. I think he must have known — he's no good when it comes to the usual doggy commands, like 'sit', and 'wait', and 'come here', but he has his own kind of intelligence.

Hunter and I cuddle for a while. I keep my head stiffly immobile. Cuddling your dog after you've been through something as stressful as having your neck sliced open is soothing, by the way.

Although while I recommend the dog cuddling, I don't recommend the experience of having part of your throat slit. Even just thinking about it makes me feel queasy and dizzy.

Just cuddle your dog if you have one, and trust me that it feels amazing to be able to do that after nearly dying.

The thought is overwhelming. I could have died. Somehow it feels more real this time around than the previous times when my life was in danger. Something about the enormity and finality of a wounded neck....

"You're awake." Tim saunters in and hops lightly up on the bed, bringing a welcome relief to my thoughts.

"I am." I smile. "Thank you for your help, Tim."

He does the equivalent of a cat shrug.

"No, really, if you hadn't stepped in to save Hunter—"

"I did *not* save that stinking furball."

"You did, Tim. You saved Hunter."

"I didn't—at least if I did, it was an unintended consequence of my actions, okay? And if you go around telling people about it, I'll deny it flat out."

I reach out gingerly with my left hand, still careful to keep my neck still, and stroke him. "You probably saved me too, you know."

"Alright, alright, enough with the displays of emotions. We're not Spanish."

"What has being Spanish got to do with any of it?"

"Well, they're emotional, aren't they?"

"Are they? I've never been to Spain. And anyway, there's no one here, so it's not a display."

"Trust me when I say that the Spanish are emotional, and I'd rather you didn't follow in their footsteps. I have a relative downstairs, so it's not an appropriate time for your emotions, okay?"

I scratch behind his ear, and he settles down on the bed, purring. "Okay, no more displays," I tell him. "But thank you."

After a time, I gingerly clamber out of bed. I'm terrified that shifting my head will cause the wound to re-open, but it holds fast. A quick inspection of the bathroom mirror shows me an odd-looking scar. It's light blue and puffy. That's what the healer meant when she said the blue had to be absorbed.

I don't dare touch it.

I head slowly to the stairs, followed by Tim and Hunter. As I start to make my way down, Hunter whines from the top of the stairs.

"I'll carry him," Sarroch says. He appears at the bottom of the stairs. "I had to carry him up. I think stairs will be a challenge for a while."

We cross each other in the staircase as I go down and he heads up to pick up Hunter. I still haven't worked out what I feel about him being here, about his help. I could be grateful, but then it was his *wife* who attacked me in the first place.

I'm tired, I'm still recovering from a grave injury, so I feel very much entitled to continue with avoidance. I ignore the whole thing.

Instead, I take a quick inventory of my living room. There are dead vines on the ground at the kitchen's entrance, and the floor is littered with flakes of brick and plaster and paint from where they burst through the walls and ceiling.

"Where's Zer?" I ask.

"She's in the courtyard. She doesn't seem to like the look of me much, so I've given her space. The rest of your animals seem to have returned out there as well. Kamlai called Sangong to notify him by the way, so the barbershop knows not to expect you today."

"That's good. Thanks," I add on second thought. I'm not ungrateful – at least I'm not trying to be. I just... I'm not quite ready to dissolve into gratitude for Sarroch saving me from the attack of his insane, homicidal *wife*.

I make my way slowly through my kitchen, plaster crunching underneath my bare feet.

Outside, the canopy of vines remains and it still covers the walls of my courtyard, stopping any moonlight from getting in. Enough light spills out of the kitchen door for me to see by.

It all looks strangely normal. The rabbits are dozing in their hutches, and the guinea pig is in his straw and newspaper lined nesting box. Fergie and Zer are settled together in a large, empty flowerpot. They're adorable, cuddling together—and they both seem fast asleep. Barung is also sleeping on a perch.

Frank the frog is the only one who is awake, sitting on his rock, optimistically singing in the hope of attracting a mate. Frank, the eternal optimist, and the eternal romantic...

Satisfied that everyone is safe, I head back inside. I'd really like to try to talk to Zer about what happened, but I don't want to wake her. It might have been draining for her to summon up those vines.

"Would you like some tea?" Sarroch asks. "I had some

specially delivered along with a teapot and cups — I didn't feel comfortable rifling through your kitchen cabinets."

It would be churlish of me to refuse, and tea does sound lovely right about now. I guess I'm not going to be able to continue ignoring the fact that Sarroch is here, in my living room.

I carefully settle myself on the sofa, Sarroch helping me with the cushions so I can lean my head back against them.

"The healer did a good job," Sarroch says. "She says that so long as you're careful for a few days, you'll make a full recovery."

He helps Hunter get up next to me. Then he goes and makes tea in my kitchen. I can just about see him through the entrance, and I have to resist the urge to move my head to keep an eye on what he's doing. I don't like people using my kitchen, not unless I know them very well. I don't like people using my things in general, because so few take proper care.

But Sarroch is moving precisely, boiling a kettle that is not mine on my stove, and then readying the tea. When he splashes some water on the counter, he wipes it down at once with a tea towel that is also not mine.

I approve of the wiping of the counter, and the tea towel is pretty, printed with a blue and white pattern of koi carps.

Sarroch brings the teapot and cups out on a tray that is again not mine. He has obviously has a whole load of stuff delivered. It's both over the top and oddly considerate.

As he reaches the sofa, I can smell the tea—smokey, black Lapsang Souchon.

He serves the tea and then sits down at the other end of the sofa. "Apiya, I would really like to explain. About Yue. I know she was the one who came here today."

All my good will over the making of the tea evaporates

like steam out of a boiling kettle. "To be honest, I'm not sure I'm in the mood to hear it." Actually, I'm not in the mood *at all* to hear it. Okay, so I am being churlish. Sue me. "What are you going to tell me — that you and Yue got married a long time ago and you've been estranged for a while, now? Firstly, that's a cliché, and secondly that doesn't excuse or explain the fact that your wife tried to kill me."

Sarroch shakes his head. "Nothing excuses that. But I figured you probably would want to know why she tried to kill you in the first place."

If I wasn't so worried about my neck, I would shrug. "Does Yue really need a reason? The fact that I'm human would seem to be reason enough for her. Unless this is some other attempt at provoking a war."

Sarroch shakes his head. "Can I explain?" he asks quietly.

"No."

I expect him to insist, try again, or just go ahead and do what he wants. After all, it's not like I can make a fast getaway. I'm very much a captive audience.

But he does none of that. He nods, looking aggrieved, and falls silent. We drink our tea for quite some time without speaking.

"Fine," I say grumpily. "Fine. If you insist, you can explain."

Sarroch takes a breath. "Thank you. I should warn you that this will take a little while."

"Well, it's not like I've got anywhere else to go."

12

S arroch clears his throat and looks down at his hands. This is definitely the most uncomfortable I've ever seen him, and in spite of myself, my curiosity is piqued. I also feel a sense of validation. At least it's not just me being crucified on the altar of embarrassment.

"The strength and power a being like me possesses is...a responsibility. As you know, given our long lifespans, we consider a Mayak to be young even a couple of centuries into their life. That's not because of the time it takes to master one's magic, but rather one's...emotions."

Again Sarroch shifts awkwardly. "You will find this interesting, actually, given the link you may well possess with Qinglong. I am unusual among the Mayak in that I am a direct descendant of Baihu."

"The White Tiger of the West?" I whisper, eyes wide. "You're a descendant of one of the Four Guardians? But how? If they have no physical body and don't come down to earth..."

"They don't. And the reason I know what would happen if one of them came down to earth is because Baihu has come down, a long time ago. He came down on several occasions, taking human form. He enjoyed...mating with human women. The results of these unions were the ancestors of today's various werecats."

"What about werewolves?"

"Werewolves are a completely different matter. Although we appear to have some similarities, their origin lies in the magic of the moon. We werecats have no ties to the moon and do not derive any power from her. Over time, Baihu's children bred with other humans, resulting in a dilution of Baihu's magic, which is why most werecats nowadays don't have much more magic than simply the ability to shift form."

"But you have abilities with metal, which is Baihu's element."

"Correct. I have a few other abilities, as well. The other Guardians didn't realise at first what the White Tiger was doing, but by all accounts each time he came down to earth it resulted in massive natural disasters – volcanoes erupting, large earthquakes, and so on. At the time the population was very small and therefore the balance in the magic was apparently easier to maintain, so his visits didn't result in total chaos. Although they did cause massive amounts of destruction. Eventually the other Guardians caught wise and forced him to stop — I am the last of his descendants.

"All my peers have now passed, so I am the last in more ways than one. One of the reasons for my long survival is that I have never reproduced. Breeding for Mayak is part of the balance—reproducing causes a weakening in the older ones, so that they may die and make way for the next generation. But for me, when I began shifting form, my mother and her tribe grew afraid of me, and they abandoned me in the wilderness. While I'm not quite immortal, it *is* difficult to kill me, so I survived. But those times were dark, lonely, and terrifying. Since there weren't many Mayak yet, it was a long, long time before I found someone like me. That was the day I met the being you now know as Sangong, and we became friends."

Sarroch smiles into his cup of tea, his eyes distant as he remembers something from long ago. Only a heroic amount of self-restraint stops me from asking him what kind of Mayak Mr Sangong is. I've always wanted to know and have never been able to find out because it is considered extremely rude to enquire about the true form of a Mayak when they have not chosen to reveal it to you.

"The terrible loneliness I went through in my young years is why I had no interest in ever reproducing. It is likely that I wouldn't live that long after having an offspring, and I couldn't find a way where I could absolutely guarantee that my offspring would never be abandoned by his or her mother. And since I had no interest in reproducing, I kept myself to myself for a very long time. Until Eyva."

Sarroch puts down his cup, looking out at an invisible point in the distance. "She was a fellow weretiger, although not a direct descendant of Baihu, like I was. We... What Yue and I have is... Well, the closest human equivalent is marriage, although it's a lot more than that—it's a bonding of our magic. But it is a rational thing, a thing of ceremony and ritual, that concerns my human form, and our magics. It does not have any bearing on my tiger. The mating of two weretigers, however, is... Far more primal. And for that reason, far deeper.

"Anyway, Eyva and I were happy for a long time. Until the day that she was captured and killed. Humans were a lot tougher, back then, and they understood about magic. We weren't quite on an even footing, but there was a type of human who hunted us, to draw magic from us. When I found that they had killed her, I... Well the best way to describe it is that I lost time. I have little memory of what happened. It was a couple of days, at most, but it was enough."

Sarroch clears his throat and looks insistently at his cup.

"So you killed the people who killed your mate," I say. He looks awkward, but that doesn't seem so terrible to me. It was a different time, back then, and you don't have to go very far back in human history to find a time when humans would have sentenced a person to death for killing another.

"I destroyed an entire civilisation, Apiya," Sarroch says quietly. "I didn't just kill the hunters. An entire culture was wiped out in a matter of days. I annihilated them all. Not just that tribe—*all* tribes sharing the same abilities. Down to the last child. Ever since that day, there are no humans left who are able to draw magic from the Mayak. I was mad with grief and rage and bloodlust, and I have so much power... I couldn't tell you the specifics of how I did it, but believe me when I say that no human genocide could ever compare to the speed and thoroughness with which I wiped out these people from the face of this planet. The only reason I was stopped before I could go further was that Sangong stepped in and brought me back to my senses."

Sarroch looks up at me. His eyes are huge, dark pools. "It is a dangerous thing," he says softly, "For a creature as powerful as me to have someone to care about. No matter that some Mayak believe I did a good thing, I ushered in a new era, a new world that was the foundation of the world we live in today. Things would have been different had there still been humans who had the ability to take magic from another. The truth is that I wiped a people from existence, and I will carry the shame of my actions with me for the rest of my life. ”

He falls silent, staring at his tea once more. I have to admit I'm not sure what I can say that won't come across as either an inane platitude or like I'm scared of him. Which... I don't know how many people we're talking about here. For Sarroch to compare his actions to a genocide...well, it's unsettling.

Especially given how controlled he seems to be most of the time.

He clears his throat again, picking up his cup in his hands and slowly rolling it between his palms. I realise I've forgotten to drink my tea and take a sip of the now luke-warm brew.

“Time passed,” he continues. “Time is traitorous. Even for someone with as long a memory as me. I realised I was tempted to forget the past. I caught myself developing feelings for another. I knew that I already couldn't bear the thought of her being taken from me. The realisation that it might happen all over again terrified me into action. That's why I bonded with Yue. She might be beautiful, and she might be intelligent, but she is also shallow and cruel, and I could never develop any kind of feelings for someone like her. A Mayak marriage is not like a human one, in that it can never be dissolved. It involves the bonding of our magical signatures in a way that is irreversible.

“Bonding to Yue sent a very clear message to everyone that I was unavailable. Every Mayak is able to sense my bond to Yue almost immediately. It also gives me a continual reminder not to fall for anyone again.”

I nod, taking all this in. I have to admit it's a bit of a relief to understand why Sarroch is married to someone as vile as Yue.

"What I didn't bank on was Yue developing genuine feelings for *me*. I should have been upfront with her about my reasons, but there was so little between us, and she's so... Well she's not exactly warm. I assumed we were on the same page. That this was an arrangement of convenience for us both. She got the connection to someone far older, more powerful, and more established in Mayak society. She was younger than me, but not that young. I didn't fully realise just how much of a romantic she was. I was distant and cold, but she took that as a sign of depth of character, of inner conflict. She somehow turned my aloofness into a challenge for her to overcome. I handled it all extremely badly. I'm not..." He shrugs. "I'm terrible at this. I should have set her straight immediately. I was a fool, and I didn't. It took time before she realised that I had no interest in her beyond the convenience of our bonding, and that I didn't, nor would ever return her feelings.

"The resulting confrontation was...ugly. I tried to pacify things by explaining about Eyva and why I don't want to have feelings for anyone else. It made things worse. I'm sure I don't need to tell you that Yue isn't someone who takes rejection well, and she is incredibly jealous. If not making my intentions plain from the start was a mistake, telling her about Eyva was my second huge mistake. We have spent the last few centuries with her stewing over her jealousy of a dead person, because there is *nothing* Yue can ever do to compete with someone who no longer exists. It's impossible to compete with a memory. She cannot outshine Eyva, she cannot kill her or outmanoeuvre her. Which brings us to the reason for her coming here today."

Sarroch clears his throat and rubs his hair with a hand, messing it up so that he suddenly looks quite young. "I enjoy your company, Apiya. I like you. You remind me a little of Eyva."

"You mean that I look like her?"

"No, not really. Not at all, in fact. But something in your way of being, in your mannerisms. She had your same ease with people, a similar uncomplicated way of enjoying life." He gives a small smile. "I'm afraid that I tend to be quite serious, and I often think... well, I overthink. Eyva was a good counter to that. And you have a similar sense of humour."

Sarroch sighs heavily. "I made a third mistake. I confided to Ari that you reminded me a little of her, and Yue caught wind of it. The fact that you are also an annoyance to her, given what happened with the egg, and the fact that you spoke up against her during the Mustering gave her a plausible excuse to attack, but I know that it's because of me. And for that, I am truly sorry. I have been careless in my dealings with Yue, and I have been careless with you. From the beginning, really. I never thought much of the Touched, and I never expected that I would come to enjoy your company as much as I do. If I hadn't been so surprised, I wouldn't have done something as stupid as mention it to Ari, when I know Yue is close to him. I should have known it would get back to her. But because you aren't a Mayak, I just didn't think that it mattered. That anyone would care..."

"Easy on my ego, Sarroch. You don't need to outline just how insignificant I am to everyone."

Sarroch grimaces. "Sorry."

"Why did Ari tell Yue, though? Didn't he realise what she would do?"

"He... She shows him a very different side. He seems to think she's a lot more sensitive than she really is. They've been close on and off for years."

"Even though you're friends? Isn't that a bit shitty from Ari?"

Sarroch shrugs. "Why? It's not like I care what Yue does, and who am I to deny others the enjoyment of another person? The problem is that Yue started her liaison with Ari to make me jealous. I was so hopeful at the possibility that she might have genuine feelings for Ari, I was thrilled. Which wasn't the reaction she'd hoped for. When I failed to be jealous, she was livid. So instead she's been doing her best to mess things up between Ari and me. We've been friends for too long for her to manage a permanent rift between us, but she does make things complicated. Ari resents me for having bonded to her. Not only have I made her deeply unhappy, but I've prevented her from ever bonding with another. Which isn't fair of me, and I acknowledge that. I think Ari would find her to be quite different to the picture she's been painting of herself if they ever could bond, but that's for him to find out, not for me to say."

Sarroch sighs. "I know it was the right thing to do, to bond to Yue and ensure I can't be a danger again. But sometimes I wish I had chosen better. Managed things better. And sometimes I wish I had never allowed the bonding to happen. But there is nothing to be done. For better or worse, she and I are linked for the rest of our lives."

13

I mull all this over. When Sarroch said he had an explanation, I hadn't expected something quite so big, quite so lengthy.

I'm also no longer quite sure how angry I am at Yue. I mean, I'm still angry at her for attacking me—that's not changing. I'm no martyr to turn the other cheek. But on the other hand, I feel a bit sad for her. What must it be like to face a lifetime of rejection from the one you're bonded to, without ever having the opportunity to end things and find someone new?

Can I admit something? I'm also relieved that Sarroch admitted he enjoyed my company, because at least it means I wasn't a completely deluded moron in my crush on him. Just a partially deluded moron—but I can live with that. I've never been too fussed about pride.

And a good thing, too, because I'm not feeling too great about how childish and shallow I've been. There is Sarroch talking of committing mass slaughter when in the depths of grief over having lost his love. Yue is trapped in a loveless bond despite the fact she quite possibly loves Sarroch, so she can't leave him and she can't make him love her back. All these big emotions with big consequences.

Me? The extent of my feelings for Sarroch didn't run much deeper than 'he looks good in a suit'...

Yep, childish and shallow. That's me. Taxi for one.

I grimace at my tea. I'm not normally that immature, but I have to admit that when it comes to the opposite sex...it's all such a disaster.

"I'm also sorry if I've misled you in any way," Sarroch says formally. "Ari...When we spoke about it, he pointed out that I should be careful not to give off the wrong signals. Which I clearly did for a long time with Yue. And I would hate to mislead you about... er..." Sarroch clears his throat again. "Magic help me, I'm bad at this. But it's best if I avoid relationships entirely, and if I gave you any other impression, then I'm truly sorry. It is just far too dangerous, for a creature as old and powerful as me to have someone to truly care about," he finishes, echoing his words of earlier.

I smile, my ego only smarting just a little. Rejection is never nice, but at this point I'm well aware of where we stand. "You're fine, Sarroch. Nothing to worry about."

He looks very relieved.

I almost ask him if this way of living isn't a little lonely, but that probably isn't a good idea. If it is lonely, I'll just be drawing attention to it, either forcing him to either lie or show vulnerability. If it isn't lonely, then there's no need to ask the question.

But it does sound lonely to me.

It's not that I believe you can only be happy if shacked up. Some people are perfectly happy on their own—case in point, me. My life works well when I'm single, and it inevitably turns into a crapshoot the moment I start seeing someone.

But it's a different matter to be alone because it is forced on you by external circumstances. And as to being married to Yue... Well, that thought in itself is shudder-inducing.

"So where does that leave me with regards to Yue?" I ask aloud. "I can't imagine she's the kind to forgive and forget, and I don't particularly want to repeat the experience of having part of my neck sliced open."

"Well...No action was taken previously for her attacks on you. You are Touched, she is Mayak, and so long as she stays within the rules of human hunting, she will face no repercussions. There were no witnesses here, no fuss, nothing to draw attention. Even your wound could be assigned to something not related to the Mayak. To punish a Mayak for attacking a human would set an incredible precedent. It's like punishing a human for shooting a deer, if the deer doesn't belong to anyone."

I open my mouth to protest, but Sarroch puts a hand up.

"I will see what can be done to change that and ensure you are protected. I am personally responsible for this situation, and I will see to it that you don't suffer any more because of my actions. But I'm not sure how it will go, and whatever I'm able to do, it will take time. In the same way that it would be difficult to universally ban the killing of any animal by humans."

"And as her...husband...or do you have another term for it?"

"I'm her..." The sounds that follow are not sounds that my tongue is able to make.

"Okay, we'll just say husband for now. So as her husband, can you not talk to her, ask her to stop? Or even make her stop? Do you have any authority?"

Sarroch raises an eyebrow. "Mayak society is far more egalitarian than human society. In our world, husbands do not have any particular power over their wives to dictate behaviour."

I grunt. "While I'm normally always in favour of equality, in this case I really find myself wanting to make an exception. The phrase 'put a leash on her' comes to mind." I take a sip of my tea and realise it has grown completely cold.

"I'll boil more hot water," Sarroch offers, standing up.

"I could get used to this," I call after him cheerfully, distractedly stroking Hunter's silky ears. "Being waited on hand and foot."

Sarroch lets out a low laugh from the kitchen. "I'm not really sure being waited on hand and foot is worth nearly dying from a wound to the neck."

"That depends. If you were to feed me peeled grapes while waving a fan, I might allow myself to be convinced."

"Hmmm, you might be waiting for a long time for those peeled grapes. For now, it'll just be tea, I'm afraid."

"Oh, the neglect." I make a mock dramatic sigh, resisting the urge to complete the look by pressing a hand to my forehead in case I move my neck. After all this serious talking, it's nice to have a beat of levity.

Once the water has boiled, Sarroch throws out the old tea and makes a fresh pot.

"Until I have been able to make progress, it would be best for you to stay home," Sarroch says, returning with the tea. Our joking has obviously come to an end, and it's back to the serious talk. "I will contact Chai so he can look out for you when I can't, and same with Sangong."

Something occurs to me, then. "Speaking of which, how was Yue able to enter my house? I thought Mr Sangong had set up security spells to stop that?"

"Yes, but he has keyed them to allow me in. My magic is bonded to Yue's, so anything that allows me allows her too."

"Oh, great."

"She's unlikely to try again here, though. Too obvious. But in time she *will* try again, no matter how long it takes before she gets a good opportunity. Our best way to stop her is have a new precedent set for you, change your status or role in Mayak society."

I nod. "Makes sense." I sigh. "What a mess." We drink our tea in silence for a moment. Something pops into my head, something a tad shallow, but that piques my curiosity.

"When you stopped Yue in the forest—you know, when the pari-pari egg was freshly hatched. I saw beneath Yue's glamour. She was old and withered, and..."

Sarroch looks sad. "She's not. A pontianak's natural form reflects her inner landscapes. When they're happy and fulfilled, they are dazzling creatures. If not, well...Feeding on humans enables them to keep the appearance they would have if they *were* happy. What you saw of Yue...She's become bitter and resentful, and she's carried anger for a long time. I'm the cause of that, too." He gives me a wry look. "I'm supposed to be wise, given my long life and the fact that I descend from Baihu, but I'm not. At least not in these matters. Not by a long way..." He sighs. "Anyway, I intend to try to make what amends I can. Chai will be able to keep you safe when I go to start arguing for something to be done to protect you."

I raised an eyebrow at him. "Wow, is that an endorsement of Chai? You never seemed to think very highly of him, and yet you think he can square off against Yue?"

"It's not him that I thought poorly of, it's a long lifetime of thinking of the Touched as irrelevant and insignificant. Their lives are so short, their powers limited... But I am prepared to admit that I may have been mistaken in dismissing you all."

"Don't forget that I may not even be Touched at all." I lift up a finger, pretending to be all lofty. "We may discover that beneath my weak magic and limited abilities, I am in fact the most powerful being in the world."

Sarroch laughs. "We may indeed. Although for your sake, I hope that's not the case. The happiest among the Mayak tend to be those like Kamlai with small powers. Powerful beings like Sangong and I don't tend to find happiness easily."

We chat some more, and after a time fall into a companionable silence.

It occurs to me then that this is the most comfortable I've ever felt around Sarroch. Maybe because I finally know him a bit better, and because I've stopped focusing on how he looks in a suit.

Shallow? Moi?

But now that it's clear there is nothing on the cards beyond friendship, it feels like Sarroch and I have reached a new, more relaxed place. It's nice. No pressure, and no expectations. No misunderstandings.

And, okay, I'm still free to admire how my friends look in a suit, from time to time... Right?

14

To say that Chai is angry is an understatement.

I wake up the following morning to the sound of a hushed argument and come down to find Sarroch and Chai standing off in my living room. Their voices are low and harsh, and Chai's fists are clenched.

The moment he sees me, he snaps out of it, smiling and turning relaxed. "Morning princess."

"Having words with Sarroch?"

"Seemed necessary, given the situation," he replies. Sarroch's expression darkens, but he doesn't protest. Chai gives him a cool look. "I'll take it from here. I think that's for the best."

Sarroch's jaw clenches briefly, then he nods. Can't be easy for a Mayak to be given a dressing down by a Touched. Good for Chai, that he got to give it.

"I'll be in touch as soon as I have any news," Sarroch tells me.

I nod. Sarroch glances back at Chai. "Be on the lookout. I doubt Yue will come back here, but she *will* try again." He hesitates. "And don't be too proud to call for help. Yue is powerful."

And then he's gone.

Chai turns to me. "Api, I'm so relieved you're okay. When Sarroch called to tell me..." His voice catches.

I get to the bottom of the stairs and give him a stiff, awkward hug as I try not to move my neck. "What were you saying about me making better choices regarding men?"

"I take it all back." Chai takes a step back and examines me critically. "You no longer have my blessing to make any kind of choice. Or even be mildly attracted to anyone. No dating for you, no flirting, nothing. I don't know how you do it, Apiya, but your love life makes mine look like a roaring success."

"I'm not sure we can call this my love life. That involves something happening between both people in question, and Sarroch made it amply clear that won't ever happen."

"So much the better. The less there is between the two of you, the better. I'm staying here tonight, by the way. Sleeping on your sofa. No, you don't get a say in it."

I smile. "I wasn't going to protest. I have a feeling that I won't be sleeping great for the next few days, so company will be welcome."

Chai's expression turns angry again. "I can't believe he let...No, no, this will achieve nothing." He takes a breath. "Mr Sangong is going to be at the initial meeting with Sarroch and he will come by later to tweak the security spells on your house."

"I should probably also tell Ilmu what happened."

"I told her already. Sent her a message."

"Oh. And?"

"No reply."

I frown. "That's odd. I mean, Ilmu isn't exactly the

warmest of people, but I'd have expected her to be at least a bit worried."

Before Chai replies, Tim calls out from the kitchen. "Someone come open the cold water tap for me."

"There's a water bowl on the floor, Tim."

"You expect me to drink from *Hunter's* bowl?"

"You're a *cat*." I'd love to say I was pointing out the obvious, but with felines, nothing is certain. "It's a water bowl. You drink from it."

"That's repugnant. Open the tap for me."

I glance at Chai and roll my eyes. "Fine, I'll pour you a fresh water bowl."

"I can do it," Chai offers.

"Let me do at least that. From what the healer said, I have a few days of being a cripple, so you'll have plenty of opportunities to fuss over me."

I step into the kitchen. Sarroch must have cleaned up all the broken plaster and brick dust. The things he had delivered—the teapot, tray, cups, tea towels, and other kitchen implements—are still there. A reminder of our lengthy conversation. Although said conversation contained a heavy dose of rejection and of me facing how childish I've been, I find I'm recalling it fondly.

Tim is sitting by the sink.

I grab a bowl and fill it with water. "Here." I place it next to him.

He looks at me like I'm an idiot.

"You wanted water," I remind him.

"No, I wanted to drink from the tap."

"Oh, for crying out loud. This is fresh water, Tim. You saw me pour it. What's wrong with it?"

"What's wrong is that I want to drink from the tap."

"You'll drink from the bowl."

This goes on for a while, much to Chai's amusement. Eventually, I decide to break the stalemate by walking away. I won't be browbeaten by a *cat,* of all things.

But as I head back to the living room, Tim begins to yowl. Loudly.

"Tim!" I warn.

"What? I'm merely singing the song of my people. In protest at the appalling treatment I'm receiving. It's a song of terrible sadness and yearning." He starts to yowl again.

"Stop being a drama queen."

Tim continues to yowl. For a long time. Chai and I chat, and I try to ignore it. I check on the animals, and I try to ignore it. I put music on, which actually only makes things worse.

Did I say I wouldn't be browbeaten by a cat earlier? Maybe we'll just pretend I didn't say that. I'm tired. Okay? I'm tired, and I nearly died. That's the only reason I'm allowing a cat to get the upper hand on me.

I open the tap and finally, blissfully, Tim falls silent.

He doesn't drink, though. No, instead he looks at me and blinks at me slowly. It's hard to remember that only recently I was feeling overwhelmingly grateful to the little bugger for saving Hunter and me.

I glare at him. "Drink, you pain in the ass."

"This reminds me of a standoff from one of those old Westerns," Chai comments. "Which one of you would be Clint Eastwood?"

"If Clint Eastwood wins, that would be me," Tim says. And then he begins to drink.

15

The next few days are an agony of boredom and tiredness. Mr Sangong comes by to tell me he's updated the spells on my house, and Sarroch can no longer enter, which means Yue can't, either.

I'm safe. For now.

Chai uses Mr Sangong's visit to take Hunter out to do his business, not that the poor love can have much of a walk with his busted leg.

Mr Sangong asks me how I managed to last so long with a wound at my neck, and I explain about connecting to my own blood and drawing it back into myself.

He gives me a small smile. "Well done, Apiya. Very well done." There's a small but unmistakable gleam of pride in his eyes.

I can't fully explain why it matters to me as much as it does, but having Mr Sangong be proud of me feels significant.

"Is Sarroch making any progress?" I ask.

Mr Sangong sighs. "It's far too early to tell. If there is to be progress, it will take weeks or months. Yue's attack on you brings to a head a number of complicated issues. The status of the Touched in Mayak society, what it would mean if a Touched is important enough to be granted special rights to protect her, the precedent that sets, and so on. But of course this then leads to humans in general, to the Mayak's relationship with humans... Big issues that need to be discussed, debated, considered... And of course the direction this goes in will have an important impact on the issue of the potential war with the Mundanes. It will take time, Apiya. Patience."

I'm dismayed. "Then what, I have to stay home until some resolution is brought about?"

"I'm afraid so. You'll be safe here, now. If you go out, Yue will very likely take the opportunity to get rid of you. On top of everything else, you're an embarrassment. She attacked a Touched who is known to have weak magic, and she failed. Getting rid of you would help with the tremendous loss of face she's suffering from at the moment. It would also make sure that all these discussions don't have an influence on the war issue. I'm afraid that if you die before an agreement is reached, there will be no consequences for her, and things will just continue as they are."

"But... All my clients at the barbershop... Doesn't that matter? And what I've done for the Mayak so far...surely that has to count for something."

"Of course it matters. That's why Sarroch is even able to bring this to the table and argue a case for you being granted a special status among the Mayak. You just need to be patient, Apiya."

Patience, which is most definitely not my chief virtue.

I do my best to keep myself from being bored to tears as the days slip by. Eventually Chai has to get back to his studio and to his work. Since no Mayak other than Mr Sangong can enter, I'm safe even without supervision, but my boredom increases exponentially.

Chai does his best to keep me entertained, coming by as often as he can. He also takes Hunter out so he doesn't always have to go in my courtyard, and he takes Hunter to the vet for a checkup. His leg is healing well.

My wound is healing too—the blue stuff on my neck slowly being absorbed. I begin to move a little more, pottering in the courtyard with my animals, though nothing too strenuous.

As if there weren't enough frustrations in my life, Tim continues to insist he can only drink from the kitchen sink tap. The song of his people comes out any time the tap isn't open the moment he wants water, and it's driving me around the bend.

He also yowls the song of his people when I don't let him sleep in my room.

Let me tell you that being woken up by a cat yowling at two in the morning isn't fun. Especially when your dreams are plagued by nightmares. The little bugger has me jumping awake, heart pounding, only to realise that I'm not under attack, it's the bloody cat wailing.

"Tim, I told you that you're not sleeping in here," I yell.

The yowling stops. "How can you be so cruel? To leave me out here alone?"

"I let you sleep in my room before, remember? You spent the night complaining about the smell of Hunter, and about the loudness of my breathing. So you don't get to sleep in here anymore."

"What happened to gratitude? I *saved* you and the stink ball."

"I thought that was an accident."

"It was, but the consequences are undeniable. Which means you owe me."

"Well, I truly am grateful, Tim, but I need to sleep. So you can sleep downstairs. Or better yet, go out and prowl. Aren't cats supposed to be nocturnal?"

The yowling takes up once more.

"Tim, I swear to god, you're driving me crazy!"

"You know the way to make me stop."

I stomp over to the door and fling it open. "Don't you have magic that allows you to slip through human-made doors, anyway?"

Tim rubs himself against my bare legs and saunters over to the bed. "I do, but in this instance I didn't just want to get in, I wanted *you* to let me in."

I think I'm in danger of bursting a vein.

Tim jumps up on the bed. Hunter glances at him without moving. He's curled up on the foot of the bed, and he sighs contentedly. I don't normally let Hunter sleep with me, but he's earned that privilege. And I find his nearby presence reassuring.

"Gah, he stinks," Tim protests.

"Stop complaining," I mutter as I slip back under the sheet. I sleep with my bedside lamp on these days, the warm light reassuring. When I wake up in the middle of a nightmare featuring crying babies in forests and monsters stalking me, I need to be able to see at a glance that I'm safe and alone in my room.

I grab a book—it's going to take a little while for me to get back to sleep.

"How can you bear it?" Tim asks as he settles himself on the pillow next to mine.

"No talking." I start to read.

Has a cat ever obeyed a command?

What a stupid question. Of course not.

Do I get any sleep that night?

Not a wink.

It's a good thing I'm stuck at home and therefore free to nap as much as I want, a privilege I intend to make full use of.

The next morning, in between shuffling, zombie-like, I go to the courtyard. Zer is playing with Ferg as usual. I try to reach for her with my magic (she's definitely back to being female), but her walls are still up, and I can't get anything from her.

In fact, since the day with Yue, it's like nothing happened. Like we've gone back to normal.

I don't really understand what brought on her extreme reaction to Yue. Was it a reaction to me being attacked? To Hunter's pain? Or did she recognise Yue from when she was a hatchling? I wish I understood more about her, and about why I can't reach her with my magic.

I'll need to get in touch with her parents to find out, but since I no longer have their tears to summon them, that would mean leaving the house.

I *miss* the outside world.

Speaking of parents, I've also been avoiding calls from my mother. I feel bad, but I don't want her worried. She's halfway across the world, and she doesn't need to know that I was sliced open by a pontianak. Also, the woman can sniff out a lie better than a bloodhound.

This time, though, when my phone rings, I pick up. I've recovered enough that I sound normal, and I should be able to say all is fine without technically lying, so it should pass.

"Why, it's the motherload!"

"Darling, what's wrong?" she asks at once.

"Hello to you too."

"I was getting worried when you didn't pick up these last few days."

"Sorry, I've just been busy."

"Darling, I can tell when something is wrong. What is it?"

See? She's like a bat. I swear if I had picked up a couple of days ago, her bat radar would have told her that her daughter had a neck wound. "I'm fine, Mum. All okay at your end? Is Dad surviving, or should I prepare myself for life as an orphan?"

"Surviving, yes. Not much more than that, though. I hired a cleaning lady to drop in on him. He was too distracted to listen to her explanation of who she was, and he had obviously forgotten that I'd told him about her, because he basically closed the door in her face, telling her he was too busy for visits. I dread to think of the state of the house when I get back."

"Think guinea pig nest, but with more paper," I say helpfully.

"Exactly. Between your father and I, it's a miracle that you turned out so tidy. We'll have to thank your birth parents for passing that gene down to you. Dad told me about that passage he found on Qinglong, by the way. And it reminded me of something. Do you know the Akha tribe who live in South Panong?"

"I know *of* them."

"Well, they believe and worship the spirit of all things— the earth, the rock, trees, sea, etc. And they believe all these spirits come from one Great Mother. It might be Qinglong, although I haven't heard them refer to her by that name. But it might be a linguistic difference. They might know something that could be useful to you."

"Mum, you're the best. That's amazing—I'll go see them."

"Good. Let me know what you find out."

"Of course."

"And you're *sure* everything is ok?"

"Everything's *fine*, Mum. Nothing's wrong."

"When you repeat yourself like that, it's because you're lying. What's up?"

"Nothing. Seriously. The only thing that's wrong is you pestering me when nothing *is* wrong." My fingers touch the spot at my neck where a faint blueish tinge remains. No scar otherwise, which is a relief. I'd have a hell of time explaining a scar at my neck otherwise.

Mum grouses a little more, but eventually she gives up the fight. For now. She's going to be checking in on me for days to come, just wait and see.

I hang up and check myself in the mirror.

The blue at my neck is so faint now, that I'm sure it'll be gone by tomorrow. Once it's gone, I should be able to convince Chai that we should go see the Akha. I need to get out of this house, but I'm not going to be stupid. If I have Chai with me, I'll be safe from Yue. Plus, it will only be a quick trip to talk to them, and then straight back here.

I try to stop myself from feeling excitement at the thought of going to see the Akha. As Mum said, it might be nothing. But then again, it might be something...

16

"No way." Chai's mouth is pressed into a flat line, his arms crossed over his chest.

"Chai, come on. This is too good a lead to pass up on."

"You're not leaving the house."

"You'll be there. You can take Yue on, right? Or are you worried that you can't?"

"Subtle, Apiya. Quite the master of reverse psychology."

"Chai, pleeeeease. I'm losing my mind, here. I *need* to get out. And this is too important to pass up on. Plus, anything I find out might have a big impact on the situation with Yue. If I can find something that confirms I'm not a Touched, that could change everything."

Chai nods, and my heart leaps. "That's true. Once Sarroch and Mr Sangong confirm that you're safe, we'll go."

"That could be *months* away."

"Better that than you being attacked again."

I huff air out of my mouth and swear under my breath. Bloody Yue, ruining everything. Chai's right, of course. I'll be far better off staying put where it's safe. But at the same time, if I just wait around for others to save me, it won't work. Yue will eventually get to me again. And dammit, I'm not the type to wilt before a challenge—the key is getting the balance right between being a go-getter and doing something that gets me killed.

And then Sarroch materialises on my phone in the form of a text message with the mother of all trump cards. Wonderful, amazing Sarroch—who might be my most favourite person in the whole world right now.

"Chai, read this." I hand him my phone, grinning.

"Heading into a meeting with the Elders and Yue, hoping to make some sort of headway," Chai reads aloud, and he looks up at me.

"From Sarroch. That means it's safe to leave the house, since Yue will be busy. Not for a long time," I add hastily. "We'll be careful. I'll have Sarroch message me the moment the meeting's done, that way we can make sure we're back home before Yue can sniff me out. And who knows, I might find out something that will help Sarroch get me some kind of status that keeps me safe from Yue."

Chai's hesitating still. So I bluff.

"Fine, then I'll go alone."

"Apiya, don't be stupid. You'd die if Yue finds you alone out in the open."

"I survived her once before."

"Barely. And then again, only because you had help from Tim and Zer."

"Even so, it's a chance I'm willing to take. I bested her once, I can do it again." Just to be clear, I have *no* intention of going on my own.

"Apiya, seriously."

"Yes, seriously. Either I go with you, or I go alone." It occurs to me that this is the kind of pig-headedness Tim displays. Finally, a benefit to come out of all the feline torture I've had to put up with.

Chai glares at me, and I recognise this as the expression I wear when Tim is being impossible. Which of course means that I'm winning, a satisfying thought.

Okay, I can kind of see why Tim does it. Not that I'd ever admit it to him...

* * *

THE FOREST AT THE SOUTH OF THE ISLAND FEELS A LOT MORE welcoming when I'm not riding into it in the depth of night. Last time I was here, I was on my own, going in search of Ari. Well, technically I had Tim with me, but he bailed on me almost as soon as we arrived.

This time, I'm sitting in the front passenger seat of Chai's car. Hunter is in the back seat, with his head stuck out the window, tongue flapping in the wind. Is there anything happier than a dog in a car?

Actually, there is. An Apiya in a car after days of enforced time at home. It took some more work to convince Chai that we should go. I really had to channel my inner Tim.

In the end the thing that swayed him was the argument that I couldn't live my life locked up in a house, in fear of Yue—then she would win by default.

Chai's car is purring away happily as Chai negotiates the sinuous curves of the forest road. This is a *great* road to ride on the bike. A car's nice, but it's no match for the tilt of a motorbike as it engages in a sharp turn, that amazing feeling as the G force kicks in...

Still, we're driving in the sunshine, and the car's eating miles in a way that feels incredibly satisfying. The foliage at the edge of the road is thick and dark and lush, the air hazy with the afternoon's humidity. It feels like the vegetation is desperately straining to crowd the road, as if greedy to recover the narrow stretch that was stolen from it.

We'll just do a quick visit to the Akha village and then head back home.

Short and sweet and safe.

* * *

WE PULL UP OUTSIDE THE AKHA VILLAGE. AT THE ENTRANCE is an intricately carved gate which is meant to keep malevolent spirits away. It's covered with protection symbols and representations of creatures I don't quite recognise.

The Akha are not Panongian. Instead, they are a hill tribe, descendants of a migratory people that mostly live in northern Thailand, Laos, Myanmar, and the Yunnan province of China. For some reason one particular tribe broke away from the rest a couple of hundred years ago and came to settle here, in Panong.

Possibly as a result of this, their culture has forked away from the other Akha hill tribes, so they have become something of a unique, tiny culture. They live mostly separate from the rest of Panong. The government made attempts to offer what they considered assistance, mostly in the form of concrete housing, modern amenities and the likes, but the Akha refused.

Beyond the gate and the simple wooden fencing is the village. Houses are built from bamboo and wood, on low stilts, and the roofs are thatched with dried teak leaves. There are a lot of teak trees in the forest, and their leaves are large and sturdy. The oils inside the leaves also help with keeping the rain and the insects at bay. The leaves are woven into panels using slender strips of bamboo, and they provide good, watertight shelter. And if a roof needs fixing, it's just a matter of gathering more dried leaves and weaving a new panel. Cheap, easy, and efficient, not to mention environmentally friendly.

Mum would approve.

Chai and I get out of the car, and then I help Hunter get out. I'm not expecting that we will be doing much walking, and he's been as cooped up as I have, so being out in a new environment with lots of new sights and smells will do him good. In fact, he immediately starts sniffing the ground and the air, clearly enjoying the change of scenery.

Speaking of smells, as we slowly make our way through the gate, the breeze brings us the smell of somebody's cooking. Something with rice and ginger. Comforting food.

Although the village is right by the road, it feels enclosed in a little bubble within the forest. The vegetation is crowding as thickly on the edges here as it was along the road.

I can sense a distant hum of magic, no doubt the many Mayak who inhabit the forest—the pari-pari, the orang bunian, and others. The Akha are somehow able to live in harmony with them. No one else lives this deep in the forest — if they don't want you there, encroaching on orang bunian or pari-pari territory can be pretty dangerous.

We disturb a couple of chickens as we walk and they scamper off, each followed by a cluster of chicks. The chicks are still tiny and fluffy—they can't be more than a few days old. The hens squawk angrily at us.

Over to the left a boy and a girl are crouching down, examining something in the dirt. Their bodies hide it from my line of sight. The girl is wearing a faded purple shift with long white tassels dangling from the waist. The bottoms have turned reddish brown from contact with the ground. Her straight black hair is in pigtails, and she's got simple sandals on. The boy is just wearing a pair of shorts and a t-shirt, both of them also faded from the sun.

To the right, a man sits on a chair in front of a house, working on a large piece of bamboo with a small knife. He glances up at us, neither hostile nor friendly, in fact, not even really curious, and then he turns his attention back to his work.

He's dressed simply—faded black trousers, a loose T-shirt, and sandals. A single silver bangle gleams at his left wrist. The Akha are known to be proficient silver workers. The Akha are also a different ethnicity to the Panongian—darker skinned and, generally speaking, they have more pronounced cheekbones than us.

Chai, Hunter, and I approach him.

"I was hoping to speak to Pahmi U Li," I tell him in Panongian.

Not all the Akha speak Panongian — a number of them only speak their own language—those who don't engage in trade and therefore don't have any contact with the rest of Panong. I'm hoping he'll understand me, because google translate doesn't include this particular Akha dialect.

The man nods, and points to the right, deeper into the village.

I thank him and we continue with our slow progress forward, Hunter limping alongside us. We spot a few people going about their daily chores.

The men are, on the whole, dressed simply for work, as with the man we saw earlier. But although the women are dressed in a similar way, they all have amazing headdresses.

I've read about this, but I've never seen the headdresses in person, and they really are quite something. I know, by the way, that visiting a hill tribe is part of the standard touristy thing to do in Thailand, but it's not like that in Panong. For starters, we have virtually no tourism, anyway. And Panongians generally don't seem to feel the need to come at gawk at the Akha simply because they have a different culture.

It's part of the reason I've never come here before. I didn't have a reason to come, and personally it would irritate the ever-loving crap out of me if people showed up at my work or at my home to look at me, or worse, take photos.

So until now I've only ever seen the odd photo of the Akha, but seeing them in person is something else. According to Mum, Akha women decorate their own headdresses, so each one is unique. The headdresses become such a strong representation of each woman, that they apparently never take them off, not even for work.

Some headdresses rise up in cone-like shapes, while others are lower, with a flat, square part to the back. All of them have brightly coloured threads of beads hanging from the sides of the headdress, while some women have added silver coins or silver balls. Others have a fringe of small silver coins lining the front of the headdress, covering the top of their forehead.

And all of them have rows after rows of colourful beads curving down below their chin, framing their faces. The beads hide their neck, the lower rows reaching all the way down to their chest.

The younger women definitely have more brightly coloured, more complex headdresses than the older women. Obviously something to do with status, maybe. I'll have to ask Mum about it—she spent quite a lot of time with the Akha, back when she was working on the forest conservation project. They live in such harmony with the forest that they have an incredible knowledge of it.

Once Chai, Hunter, and I get deep enough into the village, we reach what looks like a ceremonial space. The ordinary bamboo and teak leaf houses make way for far more beautiful and intricate constructions.

Instead of having a normal sloped roof, the houses here have these incredible roofs that curve as they reach the front of the house, soaring up to the sky at either end. The walls are made of planks of wood rather than woven bamboo panels, the wood intricately painted in patterns of red and orange and yellow.

In the middle of the square is one of the largest banyan trees I have ever seen. The host tree has obviously died long ago, the banyan spreading numerous thick trunks so that its base is as wide as a small house. Its branches are low and heavy, stretching out parallel to the ground.

Its canopy of leaves is thick, completely blocking out the sun in places, thinning out at the edges to let through diagonal slants of golden, green-tinged light.

But the thing I noticed most of all is the irresistible pull I feel towards it. It's drawing me forward as if exerting its own gravity. Its presence is stronger than anything I've sensed before. It might be the tree, but it might have something to do with the offerings around it and in its branches.

Colourful ribbons have been tied to its branches, some marked with symbols, others left plain. The ends of the ribbons flutter gently in the breeze. Against the tree rest numerous spirit houses, similar to the ones we used to bring the disturbed ghosts to rest, after Nerong had desecrated their tombs. There are also tiny shrines, plates of offerings, and pretty garlands of flowers dangling from the spirit houses or from the trunks themselves. Slender bamboo slats also dangle from bright threads of cotton tied to the branches. Prayers and offerings are written on the bamboo.

I reach out for the tree, trying to work out what it is I'm sensing. Is it the tree itself, old and powerful, beneath all the offerings? I think back to the banyan tree in Panong's Old Town, the one I pass on my way to work. This is far, far older, although I'm not sure if it's power I sense from it or something else. Something too strong for me to make sense of it.

Or is it the numerous prayers I'm sensing? The pull of desires, hopes and dreams? There is something about the sensation that feels akin to hearing a cacophony of voices. Too many at once to be able to distinguish any individual one. Yes, it's that, and the tree as well. The tree itself is beneath the cacophony, like a deep underscoring, like a heartbeat.

"Api?"

I jump and turn to face Chai. From the tone of his voice, it's obvious he's been calling me more than just this one time, and standing next to him is an old woman.

Her dark eyes watch me from deep within the wrinkled skin of her face. Her headdress is by far the most understated I've seen so far. A relatively simple black cap, with short strings of silver coins and beads dangling from either sides of her head, in front of her ears.

She's wearing a faded yellow T-shirt with smudges of dirt on it, a blue and green sarong, and sandals. She smokes a fat cigar, but one that was clearly handmade by rolling up some dried leaves. The smell of it is both fragrant and bitter — it's clearly not tobacco.

"This is Pahmi U Li," Chai says in Panongian. He gives me the faintest frown, a questioning look in his eye.

I give a minute shake of my head — I'm fine, even

though I'm scrambling to gather my thoughts. I reach down with my right hand to stroke Hunter's velvet head to help ground me. The feeling is instant, anchoring me back into the here and now. Hunter's plumed tail is wagging softly as he considers the woman before us—he's relaxed, a good sign.

"Hello, I'm Apiya," I tell the woman. "I'm the daughter of Rebecca Chapman. I believe you know her?"

Pahmi nods once. "But you are not here in the capacity of her daughter, are you?"

"No, that's right. I had some questions, and I was hoping you might be able to help me."

"Questions?"

"About Qinglong. About the spirits of things. All things." I glance back at the tree. "And about that banyan tree…" I snatch my eyes away from it as once again it starts to pull me in.

Pahmi considers me for a moment. "Very well. Come this way." She gestures for us to follow her.

17

Pahmi leads us to a small baruga, which is kind of like a gazebo on low stilts. It's made of wood with a teak leaf roof.

We all take off our shoes — I'm still wearing my usual heavy boots, although in a nod to the weather, I'm only wearing frayed denim shorts with bare legs rather than my sweltering riding leathers.

And then we climb up into the baruga, while Hunter lies down on the ground next to the stilts.

The floor is made of woven bamboo which flexes and squeaks as it takes our weight. It's unsettling as it feels like it won't be able to support us, given how thin and flexible it is. But bamboo is amazingly strong, and the floor is easily sturdy enough to take Chai, Pahmi, and I.

Grubby, thin cushions are on the floor, and the three of us each grab one and sit cross-legged. As if responding to a command I didn't notice, a young girl appears bearing a small wooden tray with three simple clay cups.

The tea inside is fragrant but bitter, the smell echoing the cigar the old woman is smoking.

"Gulung guma deh," I tell Pahmi as she hands me a cup. These are the only words I know in the Akha's language, and I'm not completely sure that I remembered the pronunciation correctly.

Pahmi gives me a small, appreciative smile, so at least I managed to communicate that I thanked her.

Chai says a far longer phrase, and Pahmi replies, looking impressed. I raise an eyebrow, also impressed. I have no idea what he said, but good on him for being able to say more than a simple thank you.

I take a sip from my cup. The tea tastes spicier than the smell suggests—almost like black pepper.

"So what questions did you have?" Pahmi asks.

I hesitate. I'm not sure it's a good idea to start blurting out the truth about what I've recently discovered about myself, but I'm not entirely sure how else to get the information I need.

"Does Qinglong have any connections to humans?" I ask at last. "Direct connections, I mean."

Pahmi looks surprised. "Qinglong? She's the Great Mother to all spirits, including humans. She has a connection to everyone and everything."

"I mean more than just that. Does she...does she ever come down to earth?"

"She doesn't need to. She is here, in everything. In all of us, since she creates all spirits." Pahmi lifts her cup. "Whether it's the tiny spirits of my cup, or the huge, powerful old spirit in our banyan tree."

"Tell me about that tree. I felt something really strong from it when I was standing next to it, before."

"You felt? What did you feel?"

I grope for the right way to describe the experience. "I could feel the tree, old and powerful, beneath...it was like a cacophony of voices. And it was drawing me in—I mean like it was actively trying to do so."

Pahmi purses her lips. "You must be one of the sensitive ones. There aren't many of us left."

I do my best to control my excitement. "Us? You're able to connect with the spirits of things?" Have I just found my people? I glance at Chai and I can see that he's thinking the same thing as me.

I mean, I don't think I'm Akha or anything. I don't look right for that. Unless I'm mixed race with Akha ancestry? That could possibly fit...

"Connect is a big word," Pahmi replies. "We can sense spirits. Some of the larger spirits, like the banyan tree. The smaller spirits, like this cup, are far too faint for our senses."

That's a bit different from me. I'm not limited by size — I tend to be more limited by how well I know the object in question, but then again as Mr Sangong made quite clear, that is only a limitation I invented for myself. If I'm able to sense things like the ketamine in Ari's bloodstream, back when I helped him get away from Nerong, size clearly has nothing to do with any of it.

"And are you able to communicate with the spirits in any way?" I ask. "You know, make suggestions, that kind of thing."

"Make suggestions?" Pahmi looks both confused and a little horrified. "Of course not. The spirits are what the spirits are. It is not for us to try to influence them or change them. They must follow their true nature." She frowns at me. "Have you been attempting to meddle with the spirits?" she asks me carefully. "To do so is a perversion, girl."

I grimace. That wasn't smart—I've got little option left but to come clean. A good thing the Akha keep to themselves, otherwise I'd have effectively outed myself. "I don't, not in the way you mean. I can't go against a spirit's true nature, not that I'd ever try to," I add quickly. "But I can… help a chair be more comfortable which is what it wants at the end of the day. I can't make the chair be something it isn't."

"So you are able to have an influence?" Pahmi asks me.

I nod. "And I can connect with any spirit, big or small." Oh what the hell, in for a penny, in for a pound. "I seem to have some kind of connection to Qinglong. When I was at Gerabang Gate, I felt an almost physical pull from it—in fact not too dissimilar from the tree. Well, no, that's not right." I frown, trying to recall both sensations. "It's like that feeling is present in your banyan tree, among a great many other things."

Pahmi gives me an evaluating look, then seems to come to a decision. "Come with me." She looks at Chai. "Please stay here."

Chai shakes his head. "I'm not letting Apiya out of my sight."

"I hope you're not doing me the insult of implying she wouldn't be safe with me? If nothing else, I'm an old woman and she's clearly strong."

"It's got nothing to do with you," Chai replies, getting up easily. "Someone wants her harm. I'll stay back, though, but Apiya stays in my line of sight."

I reach out with my magic but I can't sense Yue. "I don't think she's here." Plus Sarroch hasn't yet messaged to let me know the meeting is over.

Chai shakes his head and gives me a look that telegraphs his thoughts—don't be so naïve. Or so stupid.

Fair point.

"Fine," Pahmi says. "But please stay back."

We leave the baruga and return to the tree. Pahmi brings

me right up to it.

The pull of it is like a vibration against my skin, like a heartbeat in my ears.

I breathe in the clean smell of burning incense, little coils of smoke curling up from remaining stubs stuck in holders. Pahmi lowers herself to her knees, moving with the practiced ease of South East Asian women who have a knack for kneeling down and getting back up with a ubiquitous grace, no matter their age.

I may have Panongian genes, but my lack of grace is all British. Nurture versus nature, I guess. I sit clumsily next to her.

Pahmi places her cigar down on an empty incense holder and reaches for a small box. It's old with that smooth, almost shiny but dark patina of wood that has been handled by thousands of hands over centuries.

She lifts the lid, and it's like a wave crashes over me. I gasp. It's the same feeling from Gerabang Gate, but multiplied ten fold.

The old woman carefully lifts up a small statue of a dragon from the box. It's about the size of two palms and is carved from a stunning royal blue gemstone. A crest of rough gemstone has been left along the dragon's spine, the myriad of tiny facets glittering.

The rest of the statue is carved in astounding detail. Asian dragons are a wholly different species from European dragons. Their bodies are incredibly long, like that of a snake, but they have four legs. They have antlers and a set of long moustaches that curl up on either side of their snout, which is long, not too dissimilar to a large wolf's. Some have spikes on their crest, some have spiked tails, some have full on manes.

Oh, and very few actually breathe fire. Out here, dragons

are related to the elements of water and air. They're far more mild, gentle, and wise creatures than the oversized, cantankerous, fire-breathing creatures of Europe. Not that I'd ever tell a European dragon that to their face, you understand. I don't have a death wish.

The little statue has antlers and twin moustaches, and each scale along the long serpentine body has been exquisitely rendered.

But as beautiful as the statue is, it isn't what has me truly mesmerised. It's tugging at something inside me. Tugging insistently. I feel a pain deep inside, and it's making it hard to breathe. It wells up slowly inside me—although I'm not sure where exactly.

Everywhere. All over.

I can't even qualify it. It's like a burn, an ache, a sharp, electrical pain all combined.

"Apiya?" Pahmi's voice is low and concerned.

"I..." I can barely breathe, let alone think.

Pahmi returns the statue to the box. The moment the lid closes, the pain stops abruptly.

"What was that?" I whisper.

"Qinglong." Pahmi leans towards me. "What happened? Are you all right?"

"I don't know." I'm not even sure what question I'm answering. I place a hand on my chest, trying to remember where I felt the pain. "I felt... I don't know what I felt. A pain but so deep inside, as if..."

"As if it was part of your very fabric?"

"Yes, that's it."

Pahmi frowns to herself. Then she raises herself back to her feet from kneeling, without using her hands. It might sound like a simple move, but for a woman who looks like she's at least in her late seventies, it's impressive.

Chai hurries over. "Api, you okay? You look pale."

"I'm fine."

"She needs some tea," Pahmi says firmly.

We return to the baruga, and the further I step from the tree, the more I return to myself. The girl from before returns bearing a ceramic teapot with a wicker handle. The ceramic is black with a blue dragon painted on it.

Pahmi was right, the tea helps.

"What happened?" Chai asks.

"I connected to..." I turn to Pahmi. "Did I connect to Qinglong?" I'm sure I did, but it would be good to get her confirmation.

"I don't know. I haven't known anyone connect to her like that, without any ceremony. And normally it's not painful."

"Ceremony?"

"We have the Majil, where we make offerings to Qinglong, so we can briefly touch the mark she has left on each of us."

"A mark?" Chai asks.

Pahmi lifts her clay cup to show us the underside. "It's like a potter, leaving her mark on the clay."

I lift up my own cup, careful not to spill the tea. There, on the base of the cup, is a barely visible fingerprint.

"And Qinglong has left a kind of fingerprint on each of us?" I ask.

Pahmi nods. "On each of our spirits. And it's not just us humans, or the animals — she has left her fingerprints on everything beneath the sun. The earth we stand on, the trees around us, the leaves, the wind... All of it is animated by Qinglong's breath, all of it has her mark. I think what you felt earlier might have been Qinglong's mark inside you."

"Is it normally painful?"

Pahmi shakes her head. "No. It's normally a beautiful, peaceful feeling. A feeling of oneness with every human being, every animal, with the sea, the forest, the earth, the sky...with the Great Mother."

That is most definitely not what I experienced. "This ceremony. Is there anyway I could... Is it only for Akha people?"

"You want to take part in a Majil?"

"Please."

Pahmi considers. "Sure. Maybe the energy from the ceremony will help with whatever caused the pain."

I release a breath I hadn't realised I was holding. I was afraid it would be something that outsiders couldn't take part in.

"You'll have to bring an offering," Pahmi continues.

"Of course. What kind of offering?"

"Whatever feels right. And make a donation to our village."

"A donation? What kind of donation?"

Pahmi smiles. "Money." She picks up her cigar—I didn't even notice her coming back with it earlier—and since it has gone out, she strikes a match to light it. The fragrant, bitter smoke rises up once more.

"Oh, of course." I feel awkward at the thought of buying my way in to the ceremony.

"No need to look like that," Pahmi says easily. "Look at it as an offering of thanks to the Akha people for hosting you. The land provides much, but money comes in handy as well. And at the end of the day what is money? Nothing more than an abstract concept, an exchange of value and of energy. Money has its own spirit, you know."

"Right, of course." I'm not sure if it's my British upbringing that's got me feeling so awkward at discussing money. Must be. Panongians are really pragmatic about these things.

"Come back tonight. I think it would be best to strike while the iron is hot, so to speak."

"At night?" Chai protests. "No way."

Pahmi frowns. "I hope you're not childish enough to be scared of the dark. The most auspicious time to carry out the ceremony is at midnight, when the spirit of the dying day merges with the spirit of the new day."

"It's not safe. Api's not coming back here at night."

"The forest is perfectly safe, so long as you don't go wandering in it," Pahmi counters. "And our village is safe."

"It's not your village or the forest that has me worried," Chai replies.

"Then what?"

I give Chai a warning glance. The Akha might be isolated, but that's only out of choice, and if they decide, they can easily get to the centre of Panong. We can't be telling them about pontianaks.

"Has this got something to with why you wanted to stay close to Apiya?" Pahmi asks.

"Yes," I reply. "But we *will* come back tonight."

Chai starts to protest. I cut him off. "If I am able to connect to Qinglong, that will change *everything*."

I can see the curiosity in Pahmi's face, but she doesn't press us for any more answers, to my relief. Chai looks annoyed, and I know I'm going to be getting an earful on the drive home.

I stand up. "Thank you for the hospitality and for your guidance, Pahmi. And for the tea."

18

I had the right of it, earlier. Chai lays into me something serious on the drive home.

"Seriously, Api, have you got a death wish? Going back there at night is *inviting* trouble."

"I agree."

"Yue is very likely to come and find you."

"I know. But you'll be there, and you can hold her off, right? And then if I can connect to Qinglong, if I can show that I have a connection to her, then I can argue that I'm not Touched. In which case, Yue's attack on me will mean something and must have consequences. Otherwise, you know as well as me that Sarroch's efforts will come to nothing. There are too many who won't want a precedent to be set for a Touched to be granted a status and protection. That's a step in the direction of us being on equal footing with them. It will only deepen the division between those for and those against war with the humans, so it's in everyone's interest to let the whole thing drop."

Chai doesn't reply, staring at the road. I can see his jaw

muscles clenching. Outside his window, the green of the forest is a blur.

"What if nothing happens tonight?" he asks at last. "What if you take a huge risk and things don't pan out the way you expect?"

"They will. Something will happen—something already did happen today."

"What?" He shoots me a curious glance. "You looked pale as a sheet when you stepped away from the tree."

I take a breath and do my best to describe the sensations I experienced. It was just a few moments ago, and yet I'm already struggling to recall it with precision, everything melding together into a confused, painful blur.

"And you think it was the dragon statue?" Chai asks.

"It has to be. Everything stopped as soon as the statue was back in the box. It was beautiful—made from some kind of dark blue stone."

"Sapphire?"

I shake my head. "No, something else. And the Akha wouldn't have the means to have such a large chunk of sapphire."

"Blue topaz?"

I look it up on my phone. "Darker than that."

"Lapis Lazuli?"

"Similar colour, but it didn't have the gold streaks through it."

Chai clicks his fingers. "I've got it. Azurite."

I feel a shiver go down my spine. "The Azure Dragon of the East. That has to be it." I look up Azurite on my phone. "Yes, that was definitely it. It can't be a coincidence that I felt something so strong when confronted by a statue of Qing-long, made of the stone that's part of her title. It's proof that there's some kind of link between us. And if I can get something more concrete, this might turn out to be my best defence against Yue. I know you don't like the idea of coming back tonight, but you also have to be realistic. I can't live in my house forever, and you can't always be by my side. Neither can Sarroch nor Mr Sangong. I have to be able to stand on my own two feet in this world, and to do that, I have to matter. I have to be someone, at least in the eyes of the Mayak. And showing that I'm linked to Qinglong in some way is how I'll do that."

Chai sighs and shakes his head. "You're too good at arguing for your own good, pudding. But you can't forget that for all your magic, your body is human. Mortal. You have to look after it."

"I do. I will."

"No, I don't think you fully realise. Unless—how old are you?"

"Twenty eight. You know this."

"Hmm. I was hoping…"

"That maybe I age slowly?" I give him a side glance. This is the first time we've hinted at his age. Normally it's a topic he stays well clear of.

Chai gives a small nod never taking his eyes off the road. "The Mayak are lucky. For all their long lives, they can have partners who survive as long as them. Having people mistake your partner for your father is… It's why I don't date Mundanes anymore. But not all Touched age like I do. Api, I've lost enough people in my time. I'd rather not have to bury you too. You'll go eventually, as well, although hopefully your magic will keep you going longer than a Mundane. But the time will inevitably come—please don't bring it forward." His voice has lowered to a whisper, but he never takes his eyes off the road.

For the first time since I've known him, Chai looks old.

Old and tired. Gone is the man who winked at me when we first met and made jokes about how good his ass looks.

I put a hand over his, where it's resting on the gearstick. "I promise I won't take any risks."

Chai snorts and glances at me, and just like that the Chai I know so well is back. "Api, you do realise I've known you for some time, now, right?" He shakes his head. "Okay, you do what you gotta do. But I'm going to get the welcoming committee out for Yue, and I won't be holding back any punches. Let the Mayak decide what it means for a Touched to kill a pontianak if it comes to that. They'll probably be so embarrassed they'll have to sweep the whole thing under the carpet or admit that I'm as powerful as them."

"At the very least, you'll cause quite the stir."

* * *

BACK HOME, I LOOK AROUND AT MY THINGS. "DO YOU THINK I should bring something as an offering that's important to me?" I ask Chai. "Something I really love?"

"I don't know if I can give you advice on that. She said to bring what you feel is right."

"Yes, but how will I know it's right?"

Out of everything in my house, the thing I love most is my record player. And my records. Let's call them one large single entity that I *adore*. I worked damn hard to get the record player sounding as good as it does, and it would break my heart to give it away. And just bringing a record on its own, without anything to play it on, seems... Well it doesn't make much sense.

"Unless I get my offering back at the end?" I muse. "Not

the money for the village, I just mean the offering for Qinglong."

Chai raises an eyebrow at me. "Do you really think that's the best way to start — trying to figure out if you can get back the thing you're supposed to offer Qinglong?"

I frown. "You're probably right."

"But if you're feeling so angsty at the idea of offering your record player, then it's probably not right, is it?" Chai continues. "When she said whatever feels right, I don't think she meant that you should sacrifice something that is so important to you that you'll resent or regret it."

I feel immediately relieved. "Yes, you're right. Okay, so something else. Something that feels right..." I continue to look around at my things, but nothing jumps out.

I hear the uneven sound of Hunter hobbling out to the courtyard. I follow through the kitchen after him. Chai has helped me repair most of the damage from the vines. Well, let's be honest, here—Chai repaired the damage from the vines while I tried to help and he repeatedly told me to stop and go lie on the sofa.

Out in the courtyard, I check on the animals. All is normal. I reach out tentatively to Zer, on the off chance that something will have shifted today, but I still come up against the same wall as usual.

"I'm going to connect with Qinglong," I tell her, trying to communicate this thought through my magic as well, in case that works better.

Nothing.

"At the Akha village, in the forest." I try to send a sense of the forest where her parents are from. Nothing.

I give up.

Hunter goes to settle himself by the pond to watch the fish swim about. The fish.

Of course!

"I figured it out, Chai!" I call out. "The fish. The fish I found in the park. That will be my offering. It's got to be linked to Qinglong in some way, right, so that should work."

Chai comes out to stand next to me. "Makes total sense, since it's linked to you and to her. And it's something special."

I frown. "Although I'm bringing it in a bowl of water and it's coming back with me, or being transferred to some other pond. It's not being killed or eaten."

"You're being a bit stereotypical, Api. Given that the Akha worship the spirits in all things, and given that this is a ceremony about connection, I doubt Pahmi will kill or eat the fish."

"They eat meat, though," I reply defensively. "They probably eat fish, too. But you're probably right. I'll just tell Pahmi that there will be no fish sacrifice, that's all." I look over at the fish happily swimming in the pond. The more I look at it, the more convinced I am that this is right. "Ilmu told me that Hunter is my guide, and he's obsessed with the fish. That has to mean something."

Chai looks dubious. "I mean, you know I love Hunter, but...assigning mystical meaning to his behaviours seems... I mean I saw him licking his bum in the car, so..."

I laugh. "Yeah, well, he's definitely still a regular dog as well."

19

We pull up to the Akha village in the pitch black. This time we left Hunter at home. I agree with Chai's assessment—the chances of Yue returning are high, and I don't want him hurt.

I shiver as I open the door and step out into the night.

"We can go back if you want," Chai whispers.

I shake my head and set my jaw. "I'm seeing this through. I'm done taking Yue's crap lying down."

I reach up to touch my fingers against the smooth surface of the throat covering Chai made me from silver—kind of like a silver gorget. It's thin enough to be comfortable to wear, and I've wrapped a strip of colourful fabric around it to hide it. It kind of looks like a scarf if you ignore the frayed edges.

Call it boho chic, dah-ling.

The scarf looks a little ridiculous against the rest of my outfit—my usual mix of cropped top, ripped denim, and generally grungy appearance. Ridiculous doesn't kill, though, but pontianaks do.

It was an interesting experience, watching Chai make it.

The silver moved as if it were a living, breathing thing, covering my neck just right, not so much that it would strangle me like the silver back when I rescued Sarroch, but tight enough to offer protection. Yue won't be able to get past it if she reaches for my neck—pontianaks are susceptible to silver, at least they are according to Wikipedia. I decided it was best not to check with my father so as not to worry him.

At the entrance of the Akha village, the night is loud with the trill of insects. Beyond the gate, the village is dark, save for a glow further in. The forest feels alive around us in a way that it hadn't during the day. I can sense magic more strongly, and I wonder whether it's the pari-pari or the orang bunian. Or maybe something else.

Reaching out, I don't pick up on Yue's signature. Not that it means much. Sarroch confirmed the meeting had ended, which means Yue's back out into the world, and free to come after me if she wants.

Very little progress was made during the meeting. Lots of talking, lots of arguing, very little in the way of decisions.

"You ready?" Chai's dressed all in black. His tattoos glow so brightly, I can just about see a hint of them through the dark fabric. He's obviously found someone to top them up, but I don't ask about that. His eyes are dark, his expression intent. He looks me over. "The scarf covers the silver well. If she goes for your throat again, that will stop her, and I'll have plenty of time to swoop in."

"I was thinking that when this is done we could start a new line of clothing." My voice sounds strangled and reedy. "You know, stylish defensive-wear against pontianaks."

My joke goes down worse than a lead balloon full of bricks. Tied to an anchor. Deservedly so—it was pretty lame.

"Take this seriously, Api," Chai says tightly. "Now, come on. Let's go."

I grab the goldfish bowl from the passenger seat. Chai is already carrying all the metal he needs to protect us, if it comes to that. He will also keep a connection to the car so he can disassemble it to use for protection. And on top of the silver at my throat I have metal cuffs, metal inserts in my boots, and a belt made of metal links. Enough that if Chai wants, he can pick me up by using his magic on the metal.

I take a deep breath, exchange a look with Chai, and then we enter the village.

A stupid, slightly hysterical laughter bubbles up in my throat at the thought that I might come face to face with Yue again tonight. I find myself trying to think of a better line than my stupid clothing joke. If I die, that can't be the last thing I've said. I should say something pithy, both funny and profound.

I'm struggling to remember why I thought coming back was such a good idea.

The houses are dark as we pass them. As we close in on the glow, I can see enough movement in it to guess it's a fire. There's also music—a low chanting.

And then we step out into the open space around the banyan tree.

The fire is well away from the tree, but large enough to cause shadows and lights to flicker across its many trunks, making the tiny statues and spirit houses look like they have come alive in the night. Peppery herbs have been thrown on the fire, adding a spicy smell to the smoke.

Five old women are sitting around the fire. They play various simple instruments, chanting a slow, rhythmic song. They all have on different versions of the same black jacket —as with the headdresses, they have embellished their own jackets with brightly coloured, embroidered patterns, beads, and silver coins. Some of the embroidery on the sleeves goes up past their elbows, beautifully intricate. They also wear elaborately beaded and embroidered leggings, and as with the jackets, each woman has made her own version.

The music is simple but haunting, the chant only using a few notes, underscored by rhythmic percussions. Beneath it all, like a heartbeat, I can feel the thrum, the pull from the banyan tree.

Pahmi stands and comes to us, and I suddenly feel a shiver of nerves. As with her headdress, her clothing is more simple than the others. A black jacket and black leggings, the calves and ankles fringed with silver coins that jangle with each movement.

The only ornate thing she is wearing is a striking collar made of silver and set with blue stones. Azurite. It's the same colour as the small statue of Qinglong.

The fire flickers across her features and unlike earlier in the day, I get a sense of power from her. Nothing quite as strong as from Chai, or from a Mayak, but there is definitely something there.

I'm reminded of the shamans of old who enjoyed a close relationship with the Mayak — she would have been one of those, back in the day.

"You brought the offering?" she asks.

I nod and present her with a goldfish bowl. She frowns at it and looks sharply up at me. "Where did you find this?"

"Close to Gerabang Gate, where I felt the pull to Qinglong."

She nods. "Yes, this is good. Come sit by the fire, both of you. One of ours will go through the ceremony first, so you may see how it happens."

Chai and I sit next to the chanting women, although I go

a little bit further back from the fire, not wanting the gold-fish bowl to get too warm.

A young girl, maybe eighteen, steps out and comes to stand next to Pahmi. She's carrying a beautiful scarf, carefully folded. The scarf is embroidered in a pattern that matches the sleeves of her jacket – I'm guessing she made both. Her headdress is taller than that of the old women, and I wonder if the height has a particular meaning.

The girl and Pahmi bow to each other in greeting, then Pahmi begins to speak words I don't understand. The tone she uses sounds like ceremonial phrasing, which is probably always repeated in the same way.

The girl replies in a similar manner. Then she goes to kneel before the banyan tree. From our vantage point, we can see her side on. Pahmi reaches for the old wooden box.

I take a sharp breath in of anticipation.

"You okay?" Chai asks, looking concerned. "We don't have to go through with this. The money doesn't matter. Just say the word and we go home."

I shake my head, eyes still glued on that box. Pahmi pulls out the little statue of Qinglong. The flickering light from the fire runs over its glassy surface, making it look like it's animated from within.

Once again I feel that terrible pull, that slow blooming of pain, as if my body has suddenly realised that one of its limbs is missing. I breathe deeply, doing my best to stay focused on the scene before me.

The girl has lifted both hands, presenting the scarf to the tree. Pahmi continues speaking a steady stream of words as she slowly brings the statue of Qinglong against the girl's chest.

She gasps, and I start, expecting her face to twist in pain. Instead, her expression is beautiful, a beatific smile of peaceful joy. She closes her eyes, tilting her face to the heavens, raising her scarf higher. Her mouth is moving, although I can't hear what she's saying.

Pahmi then removes the statue, putting it away back in the box. It gives me a measure of relief as the pain stops.

The girl slowly lowers her scarf to let it rest atop a flat, wide log that seems to have been prepared for that very purpose. She stays as she is for a few moments, looking up at the tree, hands folded in her lap, breathing slowly and looking happy.

Finally, she stands up with the same fluid grace as Pahmi, and the two women exchange low words. They hug.

There's a kind of intimacy to the scene that makes me feel like I'm intruding on a personal moment.

And then the girl walks away, disappearing between two houses.

The brief peace I felt from watching her disappears abruptly as Pahmi comes towards me. "Are you ready?"

No. Not at all. The thought of a repeat of the pain I just experienced has made all my earlier bravado flee. Do I really want to prove to the Mayak that my connection to Qinglong means Yue can't be allowed to attack me without repercussion? I could just go home. Stay tucked away safely with Hunter. Play the coward. I don't really need to find out who I am, what I am, what the deal is with my magic.

Not really.

Yes, I'm feeling about as courageous as I sound. At this point, the only thing keeping me from turning tail is my pride.

"You can't kill the fish," I blurt out.

"What on earth gave you the impression that we would?" Pahmi asks gently.

No answer to that, because that wasn't my most rational

utterance. "I don't know the words to the ceremony." I sound like a whiny little girl.

"The words don't matter. I know them enough for the both of us. You saw it, it's a simple ceremony, and I'll guide you through what you need to do."

My heart is hammering in my chest like an elephant herd in a panic, crashing through the jungle.

"Or we can go home," Chai says in a low voice. "We can turn around and leave."

Ironically enough, that's the thing that decides me. My remnant of pride flares up. I've never backed down from something just because it was scary or hard. Not since I first kicked Philip Morand, the school bully, in the crotch for mocking my eyes.

I didn't back down then, and I'm not going to now.

I shake my head and stand up, picking up the goldfish bowl. Inside, the fish is swimming in rapid circles, although I'm not sure if that's due to the small bowl or due to every-thing going on. Maybe it has enough magic to pick up on the powerful link to Qinglong that exists here. Its markings look almost green in the yellow firelight.

"Let's do this," I say quietly.

Pahmi smiles. "It will be fine. Come with me."

20

"Now you can put the goldfish bowl on the ground," Pahmi says. "It will get too heavy and uncomfortable for you to hold it out in offering."

I sink to my knees slowly and carefully place the goldfish bowl on the packed earth. The ground looks almost black in the night.

My senses seem keener than normal. I'm powerfully aware of the vastness of the open sky above me, punctured with stars. Of the immensity of the banyan tree before me, the heaviness of its branches, the solidness of the earth beneath me.

Maybe this is the start of the ceremony. Maybe this means that all will go well, and that I'll have an experience similar to that of the girl.

Pahmi begins speaking the words, reaching towards the wooden box. I breathe deeply to fight off the sense of panic. Even if it hurts, I've felt the pain of being in the presence of the statue before, so I can do it again. It's just pain for a short while.

The moment she opens it, it's like nails screeching across

a chalkboard. The same pain as before opens up within me again, aching and burning and stabbing all at once, blooming out so that it's unfurling its tendrils all the way from the top of my head to the end of my pinky toes.

I gasp for breath and try to keep myself focused. I try to sense inside me the mark of Qinglong that Pahmi told me about. I can feel nothing other than the pain.

I try to reach past it with my magic, trying to connect with the statue as I would with any other object.

The pain flares up and then something gives, as if I've pushed past it. For a fraction of a second, I'm conscious of a burst of energy akin to what I felt when I was bleeding out on my kitchen floor. Like a huge breath suddenly filling me up.

Except that it's like trying to drink the entire ocean in a single gulp. The vastness of it — whatever it is that I am touching — is overwhelming me, filling all my senses, my breath, my mind, until I can perceive nothing else but the awful sensation of drowning in immensity.

I want to lose myself in it. Drown myself in it, and yet I can't, not fully. The pain digs its talons into me, holding me back.

There's panic. Screaming. Something is thudding against my chest so fast it is in danger of either smashing my chest or itself.

And yet at the same time I'm deaf and blind and dumb, unable to breathe, to touch, just drowning, drowning, drowning. I can't move. I'm no longer in my body. It's gone rigid from the shock and pain and too muchness of it all, and I can't do anything to move it.

I'm dimly aware that my right hand is now cold and wet. Hearing returns to me.

"She's not breathing! Why the hell isn't she breathing?"

"Anchor yourself, Apiya. Anchor yourself."

Something cold and slimy slips into my hand. My fingers close around it of their own volition. I no longer have any say in what my body does, too consumed by the vastness, the enormity, the pain, the everything...

My lungs suddenly open, taking in a deep, ragged breath, but I'm observing it from a distance, not in my body at all.

Then my lungs breathe out. And again they breathe in.

"That's right, that's right. In and out... Good, Api, keep breathing."

I'm suddenly aware that the slimy thing in my hand is the fish. As soon as I understand this, I reach a beautiful moment of perfect balance. The fish, the cold, the water, they are all anchors to the earthly world. I am on earth. I have a physical body. A real body.

And yet at the same time I'm flying high overhead, at one with the vastness that I am somehow touching. I'm present with both, I can be with both without being torn apart.

For one brilliant instant, I feel a level of thrill and joy unlike anything I've ever experienced before.

I have missed you.

I don't know if the thought came from within me or outside of me.

And then I hear the soft cry of a baby before I'm flung sideways like a puppet, crashing to the ground.

* * *

I COUGH AND WHEEZE, SLOWLY ROLLING ONTO MY BACK, desperately trying to get some air back into my winded lungs. When I taste the metallic tang of blood in my mouth, I realise that I'm fully back into my body.

My head is spinning, and my left shoulder hurts, although not in a way that indicates anything serious.

And then I realise that there's screaming, both human and inhuman.

I scramble to my feet as fast as I can.

The Akha women are on the other side of the fire, all of them clinging to Pahmi who is lying on the ground. Her leg is badly burnt.

Yue and Chai are facing each other, fighting with such speed I'm having trouble figuring out what's going on. Yue screeches, an awful, inhuman sound, lashing at Chai repeatedly. But each of her movements is matched by the sweep of one of the numerous shards of silver floating in front of him, forcing her to duck and weave to avoid contact with the metal, forcing her to interrupt her attacks.

The silver shards form a kind of protective, swirling wall of protection between Yue and us.

I realise that the silver at my throat is gone, as is the silver from the women's headdresses.

Chai's face is streaming sweat, his eyes pinned on Yue. Again and again she lunges, so fast her movements are a blur, and each time he blocks her.

I feel a pulse in my left hand, as if the silver beneath my skin is responding to Chai's magic.

Yue stops her attacks abruptly. She walks back and forth in front of the silver barrier with the deadly grace of a panther. She's dressed in a skintight leather catsuit, her ink-black hair cascading down her back in a silk waterfall that blends with the darkness of the night.

"What happens if I keep this going for the next hour?"

she asks Chai. "For the next two hours? How long can you hold out, little Touched?"

"I can hold," Chai says tightly. But his tattoos, which were glowing so bright when we first arrived that I could almost see them through his clothing, are now too dull for me to make out. They won't be drained yet, but they won't hold forever. And then what?

"What do you want, Yue?" I ask. My voice sounds hoarse, as if I haven't used it in a long time.

"I would have thought that was obvious. I knew you were weak, I didn't pin you as stupid as well. Come to me and I leave them all alone."

"No way," Chai replies.

I suddenly feel a tightening of my throat, as if an invisible hand is throttling me. This isn't the first time Yue's done this to me — she attacked me this way back at the Crane, and Sarroch wasn't even able to tell what she was doing.

The squeezing sensation worsens. Chai looks unsure, quickly glancing from Yue to me, but he can't afford to remove his attention from her or the silver.

My vision is starting to get patchy at the edges. I open my mouth, but I can't make a sound.

"Api, everything okay?" Chai calls, still looking at Yue. "Yue, what are you doing? You're doing something, aren't you?" A few silver shards suddenly merge to form a stake, darting towards her. She dodges, but barely, still keeping her eyes on me. She's much slower than before, probably because of what she's doing to me.

I stagger to her.

"Api, what—"

I shove past Chai, the silver harmlessly giving way to me. Yue and I are still staring at each other.

I tear off my left glove and snatch her hand. She doesn't

react, looking confused. I reach for the silver under my skin and shove it to the surface.

Yue lets out an earsplitting scream. She wrenches herself away and leaps back several yards.

The force of it sends me crashing to the ground, but my throat is freed.

I cough and splutter. Chai rushes to my side. "Api, are you okay?"

I nod and look up at Yue. She seems to shimmer, her appearance briefly rippling. If it's possible, she becomes even more beautiful, even more flawless. But the ugly red welt at her wrist where I touched her remains.

She looks at it, aghast, and her head snaps towards me.

"Come close to me again and I'll touch your face," I tell her.

She gives me a nasty smile. "I don't need to be close to you to kill you."

"No, but you do need to look at me, don't you? Otherwise you'd have finished me off back at my house. You couldn't do that because the vines were in your way. And you can't focus one me if you're busy avoiding Chai's silver."

Her smile turns to a snarl. I've never seen anyone look at me with such hatred before. Chai's obviously got my meaning because he lifts both hands...

And then all sound stops abruptly. The air turns thick and heavy. The silver remains frozen in space.

I look around me, uncertain. Chai's also frozen, his mouth half open as if about to speak. The Akha women are looking at us, perfectly still.

Yue, however, can still move, as can I. Has she frozen time, or is this something else? Can she hurt me here?

"What have you done?" I ask.

Yue watches me silently. I stare back at her, willing my pounding heart to slow, hoping I'm not stinking of fear.

"How do you do it?" she asks at last, her voice low and muffled. "You tell me how you do it and I will let you all go."

"What have you done to Chai and the others?"

She shakes her head impatiently. "Nothing. He is fine — they're all fine. Tell me how you do it, and I stop it all. I never bother you again."

"How I do what?"

"Magic help me, stop playing dumb. You know exactly what I'm referring to. How you manipulated Sarroch."

I look at her, bewildered.

"You have him moving mountains on your behalf when you're nothing. No one. He's going all the way to the Elders in some futile attempt to keep you safe. How? How did you get him to do that for something like *you*? What trick did you use?"

"I..."

"Tell me and not only will I leave you alone, but everyone you care for. I'll make sure you're protected. Just tell me how."

I'm suddenly weirdly aware that there's too much saliva in my mouth, and I swallow. "I don't know... I'm not sure—"

Her voice turns icy. "You don't get to keep this from me. Tell me now, or I swear, none of you will survive to see the sunrise. Did you find someone with a mind magic powerful enough? Someone in Europe maybe?"

"Yue, I swear, I haven't done anything. I don't..."

"Enough!" Her voice cracks like a whip. "You will not make me believe that Sarroch cares about you. You have done something, and I *will* find out what."

Our eyes meet, then.

"Sarroch doesn't love me," I say slowly, carefully. "I don't think he has romantic feelings for me. But I do think he cares for me. In fact, I know he does."

"No, I won't believe it." Her expression has turned pained, and the anguish in her voice is unmistakable.

There's clearly no more doubt about her still having feelings for Sarroch.

I shrug. "It's true, though."

Yue's face crumples. "But you're nothing," she whispers. "You're insignificant. Why..." She doesn't finish her thought, but her meaning is clear. *Why you and not me?*

I would never have expected that Yue could look so heartbroken.

The worst part is that it's not even as if Sarroch is madly in love with me or anything like that. Quite the opposite, given his speech a few days ago. But I matter enough that he's willing to go to the Elders to try to keep me safe. And from what I saw of the two of them at the Crane, it's clear Sarroch doesn't even like Yue.

"You're not even that pretty." Her voice is small, like that of a child.

"Sarroch probably cares about you too," I say awkwardly. "I just don't think he's able...or rather willing...to be involved romantically...in that way."

Yue turns away and when she looks back at me, she's every inch the beautiful, deadly, nasty piece of work I've gotten to know so well. Her eyes glitter hard. "No, he doesn't. He made it amply clear at the meeting today. You are more important than me." She takes a shuddery breath, her face composing itself into her usual cold expression. "Well, if you have nothing of use to offer me, I guess there's no reason to leave any of you alive."

21

"Wait, what if I can help you?"

"Help me?" Yue sneers.

"Yes."

I scramble for an idea, for something to say. For all that Chai is powerful and amazing in what he can do with metal, the strain of standing up to Yue was already showing before this hiatus, and I don't know how much longer he can keep it up. Not to mention the fact that the rest of the village are all Mundanes, and therefore completely vulnerable right now.

It also is not lost on me that by coming here tonight, I put them all in danger. Nor has it escaped my notice that until now I was far too self-involved to think of that, too focused on my own safety, something that makes me feel quite seriously ashamed. And I will beat myself up over it later, but for now I need to pull something out of my ass, double quick.

"I know you think of me as little more than an insect," I say slowly to buy myself precious seconds, "But hear me out. Surely, by now, you've seen that I'm capable, and that I can make things happen. I'm more capable than you or any Mayak gives me credit for." Except Mr Sangong. I keep that to myself. "I have Sarroch's ear," I continue. "He listens to me. Not all the time, but he does consider my opinion." I hope I'm not stretching the truth too far, now. "What if I can help change his mind about you?"

Yue makes a dismissive noise. "You have no mind control magic, and in any case, Sarroch is immune to it, at least from any Mayak in Asia." The way she says it, she's obviously tried.

"Has it occurred to you that mind magic is probably not the best way to get someone to care for you? Scratch that — it's probably the worst way to go about it."

Yue's face darkens, which causes the little hairs on my forearms to stand to attention.

"I'm only saying there are other methods," I say quickly. "Methods that I can help with."

She shrugs her slender shoulders. "Maybe I don't actually care, and I'd rather have the entertainment of killing you tonight."

"We both know that's not true," I whisper.

For a moment she looks at me with such hatred that I feel it like a slap across my face.

"I can help," I reply, unable to come up with anything more. "Let me try."

Yue stays silent. The silence stretches on.

"Just let me try. Okay? If I fail... Well, if I fail, you'll still get to kill me, won't you? What have you got to lose? We both know that if you really want to kill me, eventually you'll manage it. Leaving me alive a little longer costs you nothing, but might provide you with some advantage."

Let's be clear, I have absolutely no clue what the hell I can do to help Yue. I've not suddenly grown deluded enough to think I can influence Sarroch like that. But right now, I would happily promise to bring her Shiva's chariot of fire if it means I can convince her to leave the village unharmed.

I'll just deal with the consequences of the promises I make later, when everyone is safe.

Yue hesitates. "If you fail..."

"Yes, yes. Terrible, painful, gory death for me. Fear not, I got that message loud and clear when you ripped part of my neck open. So, do we have a deal?"

Yue flicks her hand, and I sag from the shock as air, smell, and sound come rushing back in. The trilling of night insects. The crackle of the fire. The peppery smell of the smoke.

Chai stumbles, his silver shards moving as one with him. They miss Yue. He realises that something has happened, and he pauses, looking over at me.

"We have a deal," Yue tells me. She glances lightly around her, once more perfectly beautiful and composed. "But if you fail, it won't just be you paying the price. Don't think that being in Europe protects your parents."

And then she leaves with such speed, she's little more than a blur.

"What the hell happened?" Chai asks me. "Why did she just announce you have a deal?"

"Turns out she can stop time — or whatever it was that she did. She and I had a chat. I'll tell you about it later." I turn towards the fire, towards the Akha women.

They have some serious sang-froid to still be here, to not be screaming or freaking out, or losing their mind. They saw Chai and Yue fight, and they saw Yue disappear.

"I think I need to explain..." I begin.

Pahmi gestures for the other women to help her to her

feet. "Pontianaks don't normally disturb us," she says calmly. "Our gate is sufficient to keep them at bay. This one must have had serious motivation to force her way through."

I gape at her.

"You know about the pontianak?" Chai asks.

"Of course we do. You don't live in this forest for as long as we have without interacting with the spirits that inhabit it. They helped us build our gate to keep the dangerous ones at bay."

I shake my head. "I'm so sorry. I never should have come here. I knew there was a chance she'd come after me, but it didn't occur to me that she might be a danger to all of you. I should have thought of that. Coming here was stupid and thoughtless of me."

"The spirits do what the spirits will," Pahmi replies.

"What happened to your leg?" Chai asks. "Was it me, during the fighting? I was so focused on Yue that I didn't..."

"No, no. The fire flared with her arrival and it caught the edge of my trousers."

"I'm so sorry," I repeat. "I never should have—"

"If you want to help, you can increase the size of your donation to the village to cover the costs of dealing with my burnt leg."

"Of course," I stammer. "I'll cover your hospital bills. Or in fact I know of a healer who might be able to help. I'm not sure if she'll come all the way out here, but—"

"We don't use hospitals, here, and we have our own healers. We have our own way of doing things, but there are still costs involved. As I said to you before, money is appreciated as an exchange of energy." Pahmi smiles, although she looks tired and is in obvious pain. "And now before I go to be seen to by our healer, I must know. What happened, with Qinglong?"

"Yeah," Chai echoes. "What happened?"

At the mention of Qinglong, I look back towards the tree. "No..."

The fish has long ago stopped flapping. It lies on its side close to where I landed, mouth open, its one visible eye still. Its markings have turned dull, more reminiscent of a normal fish.

I go crouch down next to it, reaching for it with my fingertips. Then I reach for it with my magic, but there's nothing. Nothing at all. Less than in a rock or a branch. A deep wave of sadness washes over me.

I still don't fully understand what that fish was about, but it was a link in its way to Qinglong.

I hear a shuffling at my side and look up to find Pahmi, supported by two other women. Her leg looks both worse and not as bad up close. It's an ugly burn, but she should heal from it.

"What happened?" Pahmi replies.

"I...I'm not sure. There was so much pain, and fear, and...It was like I was trying to drink all the ocean, or breathe in all the air. It was overwhelming. Has it been like that for anyone else?"

Pahmi shakes her head. "No. We can feel our marks, safe in the knowledge that the Great Mother is in all of us, but we don't *connect* with her."

"Is that what I did? Connect with her?" I ask.

"I think so, from what you describe. You shouldn't attempt it again. Your analogy of trying to drink the whole sea is right. Connecting with something so much vaster and more powerful than us is..."

"Foolish."

Pahmi gives me a small smile. "Indeed." She sighs. "And now, I think it would be best if we all went to our respective homes for some rest. But when you can, I'd appreciate another visit from you, Apiya. We are always hungry to learn more of the Great Mother and the spirits who share this world with us. And I think there is much we could learn from you."

22

B oth Chai and I make a very sizeable donation — Chai even more so than me. I'm not sure whether he normally carries that much cash with him, or if he got it ready for today, but either way I'm grateful for it. Paying money does very little to assuage my guilt, but at least it helps to do a little something to make things right.

As we head back to the car, I vow not to return to the Akha village until I am one *hundred* percent certain that neither Yue nor any other nasties will follow me here. I would really love to come back and talk to Pahmi about all that happened, but I won't put her or anyone else in danger.

Chai and I drive off. I'm cradling the goldfish bowl in my lap. Only a small amount of water remains after it tipped over during the fighting. I've returned the fish to it and it floats sadly, belly up.

"So what happened?" Chai asks.

"I was going to ask you the same thing. I was out for a lot of it."

"Well, how about I tell you what I saw, and you fill in the blanks?"

I nod. "Good plan."

"When Pahmi brought the statue close to your chest, you basically went rigid. Your back arched, you opened your mouth like you were screaming — but you didn't make a sound. And you just stopped everything else. No breathing, no blinking, nothing. You were completely frozen. It was like your body had stopped functioning. It was one of the most frightening things I've ever seen. Pahmi grabbed your hand and shoved it into the fishbowl, telling you to anchor yourself, or something like that. I was no use, I totally panicked." Chai lets out a breath. "And then Yue was here. I have no idea where she appeared from—I was too focused on you. So I flung you out of the way and pulled all the silver to me. I'm guessing you know the rest." Chai glances at me. "You really scared me, Api."

I give a nervous laugh. "I scared myself. To be honest, I'm not sure what happened. It was just... The pain was immense—"

"What pain?"

"I'm not sure. It was like... Like my body had suddenly realised it had lost a limb. I thought if I reached the statue and connected to it with my magic that might help... Instead, it brought that feeling I described earlier. Like I was trying to drink the entire sea. What Pahmi did with the water — that helped. And I think I held the fish at some point, and when I did, everything suddenly balanced, for a quick moment. And I heard a voice. I wasn't sure at first, but now I'm definitely sure it came from outside of me. From someone else."

"Saying what?"

"I've missed you."

Chai is silent for a beat. "What do you think that was about?"

"I have no idea. The whole thing is... Utterly bewildering. But I think it either was Qinglong or something related to her. The fish had a link to her, and I only found my balance when I was touching it. Plus, the pain was brought about by closeness to a statue of her. All of this is clearly linked to her, although I don't know how."

"Well, whatever it is, I don't think I ever want to see you go through that ceremony again." Chai huffs out a breath. "Seriously, Api. Remember what I told you about your body being human?"

"As is yours."

"Yep. And I don't run around trying to connect with vast celestial beings that cause me to stop breathing. I stick to what I know—namely manipulating metals. Speaking of which, what happened with Yue?"

"Oh, that." I shake my head, already regretting what I promised. "I don't know how I get myself into these situations, but I somehow promised that I will change Sarroch's mind about her in exchange for her letting us all live today." I decide not to mention that if I fail, I die. There will always be time to bring that up later, and Chai's been through enough for now.

"How the hell are you going to do that?" he asks.

"I don't know. I don't even think that's possible." I sigh and sink back into the car's leather seat. "But let's not talk about the next crisis on my horizon. I'll deal with that later. For now, I'm just glad that we're alive and driving home. Let's focus on the little wins."

We drive in silence for a time, the road whizzing past in the light of the car's headlamps. The car's presence is comforting — I'm able to sense her more powerfully than before. I can sense her metal body, her leather seats, her purring engine, and at the same time, the whole of her.

I frown. It's a *lot* more detail than before. I turn to Chai. When we were talking I was distracted, but now... I've always been able to sense him, but somehow, things are different.

"What?" he asks. "Why are you staring at me?"

"Hold on... Just..." I frown and focus on him. I can sense the whole of Chai — Chai, my friend, as an entity. The spirit of him. The qi of him.

And yet I can sense his magic as a separate thing from him. As if it has its own qi. And if I focus, I can sense other parts of him, too. If I really focus, I can sense his blood, the air in his lungs, his heart... His memories, his thoughts... Each one a small entity, all of it coming together to form Chai.

"It's almost like... Like with binoculars or a microscope," I say aloud. "You know, how you can change the focus so you're either focused on something in the foreground or further away in the distance? It seems I can do the same. I can either sense you as a whole person, or I can dive into the components that make you up. Like I can sense your emotions, there. And over here your thoughts..."

"Don't tell me you can listen to my thoughts," Chai says with alarm.

"I'm not sure. I don't think so, at least not right now. But I can sense that they're there."

"So somehow everything that happened tonight shifted your powers."

"Not shifted. I think I've always been able to do that. Remember how I was able to just connect with the ketamine in Ari's body, but not Ari himself? It's like that, just more controlled, more powerful."

"But it's still a change in your abilities—or maybe rather a change in your skill with your magic. Do you think that will be enough to prove your connection to Qinglong? If you can show that you connected with her in some way, resulting in a growing of your magic..."

"Maybe. Hopefully. I'll ask Mr Sangong about it."

I lean back against the leather seat, listening to the car purr as Chai drives her around the bends of the forest road. I'm almost too tired from the night's events to be excited at this new development in my magic. In fact, scratch that. I'm definitely too tired.

But come morning, oh, I'm going to be seriously beside myself.

* * *

As predicted, the following morning I'm practically jumping up the walls from the excitement of discovering this new shift in my abilities. I'm literally running around my house, connecting my magic to everything, feeling all the depth and layers — or in some cases the lack of layers.

I connect with Fergie, picking out, amongst all the things that make him who he is, the determination to go up, up, up, as high as he can.

I pick him up and set him down on top of my head so he can look at his little world from the vantage point of five feet and four inches of height. I can sense that this somehow makes him happy. Where this desire to go up comes from, I don't know, but I decide that I'll carry him more often. Maybe even eventually make him a little platform, although it would need to have Fergie proof railings so he doesn't fall or try to climb higher up the wall somehow.

I try to connect with Zer, but she looks away from me shyly. With her, I get something completely different. It's like I can guess at a hint of something vast, something deep and green, something that brings to mind dark loam on a forest floor, the cool, still water of a pond's surface hiding its depths, the stillness of rocks inside a cave. But I can't go beyond that. She's keeping me out, somehow.

I don't insist. "You're a little mystery," I tell her. "One day I will solve you." I smile at her, but she continues to look stubbornly away.

I focus on Hunter, next. It's like diving into a golden pool of happy light. Not that I expected to find any darkness within him.

When I sense the broken bone of his leg, and his body's attempts to fix the break, I gently, gingerly nudge it forward, giving it what little boost I can. I keep a careful eye on him, watching for any signs of pain or distress, but he seems to be oblivious, enjoying the belly rub I'm giving him at the same time. I send a little more encouragement to help with the break's healing and then move on.

I continue to feel my way through Hunter, sensing through his memories and the simple joy that basically makes up most of him.

Having said that I didn't expect darkness inside him, I actually stumble across something. A dark patch. From the feel of it, I guess this is from when he was abandoned, when I found him. It may be dark, but it also feels peaceful, and from the way Hunter is presenting up his belly and grunting, he's not overly troubled by his past.

"If only we were all as good at moving on as you are," I tell him, scratching the spot that makes his back leg kick in reflex. Like if Yue had been able to move on from Sarroch. Things would be a lot more simple, then. Instead, she's stuck yearning for someone who doesn't want her and as a result, she's causing a lot of collateral damage.

I push that thought away. There will be plenty of time

for me to deal with that can of worms later. Actually, scratch that—it's not a can. It's a shipping container full of worms and other wriggling nasties, and it's right on my doorstep. Lucky me.

I turn my attention back to Hunter, to the dark patch I found. I'm about to move on from it, when I sense something else next to it. Something that strikes me as foreign, in a not-Hunter way.

It brings to mind the potter's mark Pahmi showed me on her cup, except that this is not a maker's mark. It's something else. Hunter is a dog, not a magical being, not a creation. Is this Qinglong's mark? It doesn't feel right for that, though.

I reach for it gingerly, connecting with it. I'm immediately flooded with a sense of Ilmu.

What the hell?

I grab my phone and call her — no reply. I try a few more times before sending her a message asking her to call me back urgently.

She told me Hunter was my guide. Has she done something to him? Is that why he's my guide? Why he found the fish? What did she do to him, and why?

I wait by the phone, but like so many before me have discovered, staring at a phone doesn't cause it to ring. I check it repeatedly to make sure it has signal, that my notifications aren't off. But a couple of hours go past, and I don't hear from Ilmu.

Unable to wait any longer, I message Mr Sangong and ask if he can come by to see me. He and Ilmu are both affected by the spell that keeps them quiet, unable to tell me anything about myself, so he might also have something to do with Hunter.

Not only that, but I think I might have an idea for how I could potentially go past the spell.

23

W hen Mr Sangong arrives, I barely let him walk in through the door before I have him sit down on the sofa.

"You want to hear about how the meeting went with the Elders?" he asks, frowning at my impatience.

I shake my head. "No. Well, yes, I do. But later. For now, I have something more important to do. Chai took me to the Akha village last night. They have a statue of Qinglong made of azurite, did you know? I took part in a ceremony supposed to help us connect with the mark Qinglong leaves on all of us. A Majil ceremony."

Mr Sangong is staring at me intently, but he remains silent.

"The ceremony didn't go well. I was in a lot of pain, I was completely overwhelmed by what I think was a connection with Qinglong herself. That may not be possible, but I'm not sure what else it could be. And I heard a voice telling me that it had missed me. Come to think of it, I couldn't even say whether the voice was male or female. It just was."

I take a deep breath, realising that I said all that in one

breath. "Anyway, since last night, my magic has shifted. It's like I can see the component parts that make up a person or creature. I could sense Chai's memories, and the blood in his veins. I could sense my tortoise's desire to get higher up, and Hunter's old heartbreak when his previous family abandoned him. Each one has its own tiny spirit, and together they all make up a whole person or creature. And then I found something in Hunter that feels like it belongs to Ilmu. And it got me to thinking... I want to sense out for your memories. You can't talk to me about my magic or where I come from, but since you *know* this, maybe your memories will tell me."

Mr Sangong smiles widely and again there is that gleam of pride in his eyes.

It really does make me feel funny to see him proud of me. A little bit like the first time I read a book about mythology as a kid, and my dad was beside himself with pride. Only Mr Sangong isn't my dad.

Right?

Suddenly I have a huge moment of doubt. What if that's it? What if Mr Sangong's my biological father? And then I realise the stupidity of what I'm thinking. He's an old, powerful Mayak. I wouldn't be human if I was his daughter.

That is what's known as clutching at straws.

I clear my throat. Since Mr Sangong hasn't said no about me looking into his memories, I reach tentatively forward. "I won't sense for anything other than what concerns me."

"I trust you."

I've already resolved that no matter my curiosity, I won't try to see what kind of being he is.

I reach his memories right away, and the feeling of vastness has me gasping. It's nothing like the vastness I confronted last night, during the ceremony, but it still...

Wow...I suppose that's what happens when you are dealing with such an old being.

I don't even need to look before a part of the memories eagerly springs towards me.

"I give you permission to look," Mr Sangong says, his voice simultaneously quiet to my ears and powerfully loud as it echoes inside my mind. His memories open before me, like a book.

And then I see him. He looks exactly the same as he does now — down to the same suit. He's in the barbershop, prepping his razors when she comes to him for help.

It's not exactly as if I see a conversation between Mr Sangong and Qinglong. Not really. Rather, I suddenly gain an awareness of what she communicated to him. Of her terrible loneliness for millennia and millennia. Of the indifference of the other Guardians of the skies. They don't have the same connection to all living things as she does. They don't crave contact with another like she does. And when she suggests to them that she could go down to Earth briefly, like The White Tiger of the West did long ago, they shut that idea down at once. Too much potential for instability. The world is too large now, too complex, with too many moving parts.

So instead, she begins to steal. Tiny fragments. Minuscule. Infinitesimal scraps of qi. She is the one who brought qi to the world and animated it, so in a way it's all hers, anyway. She takes a first scrap back to her, and then another. More and more she steals, her little hoard growing and shifting and taking form, until there is enough there for a small being. A being that is hers and only hers.

If she animated the whole world, why can't she animate a daughter for herself? There's plenty to go around. I get a sense of her deep, deep joy at having someone that is all hers. She hides her tiny daughter in the crook of her elbow, guarding her jealously.

The memory moves quickly on.

The other Guardians realising that the world has fallen hopelessly out of balance. It had started so slowly they hadn't noticed at first. Humans starting to turn away from the Mayak. Humans choosing to focus on technology and science, deviating from the path all living creatures were on.

It grows worse and worse, the more Qinglong takes. War engulfing the whole planet. Pollution poisoning everything. Wholesale destruction.

The other three Guardians finally figure out what Qinglong has done, how she has selfishly taken from the world, causing it to slowly, gradually fall into complete disarray.

I sense how they order her to destroy her daughter and return the stolen qi to earth in the hope that it would restore a measure of order. How they ignore her desperate pleas to let her find another solution so she can keep her daughter.

And then the memory returns to the barbershop, to Mr Sangong standing in the middle of it, apparently alone. His eyes are closed. Qinglong is asking him to help her at least keep her daughter whole. The qi can return to earth to help restore balance, but Qinglong doesn't think that ripping a being apart, however tiny, will help with the chaos.

Better that her daughter stay whole on earth, her qi helping to balance out the energies.

The memory moves to Mr Sangong stealing a tiny corpse from a hospital. A human newborn whose mother died in childbirth before she could take her first breath, so the baby died too.

Human bodies have magic to them, it turns out. If the brain is absolutely convinced of something being true, then it will make it so. If a body believes itself to be dead, nothing can keep it alive. And conversely, if the body believes itself to be alive, so it will be.

Qinglong deposits her daughter inside the baby. And then I watch as Mr Sangong takes her to Sarroch's house, seeking help, although I can't quite see what for. Sarroch is out, and Mr Sangong waits in Sarroch's living room for a long time. Sitting on the daybed I recognise. The daybed that responded so eagerly to my presence.

The baby in Mr Sangong's arms is very much alive now, but she's far too alert for a newborn. Because of that, no one would mistake her for a human baby.

Mr Sangong gives up on Sarroch and brings the baby to Ilmu. It takes some convincing, but she agrees to help and devours the baby's every last memory, wiping the slate clean — as it would be for a real newborn. The unnatural alertness she had fades away until she looks no different from any other newborn.

The memory shifts again—Mr Sangong keeping an eye on her from afar, watching as my parents come to the orphanage, as they take me away.

And then the memory ends abruptly, in such a way that I'm pretty sure Mr Sangong was controlling what I saw.

Released from it, I sag back against the sofa cushions, too overwhelmed to speak.

"Apiya?"

I shake my head dumbly. "Give me a moment." It all fits though, doesn't it? The fact that Meng Po told me that I am an incarnated soul, that I had no physical body before. Even my magic—it's all about connecting with the qi of things. The way I appeared suddenly at the orphanage, without a record. Sarroch's house responding to me so strongly, probably because I was brought there before my memories were removed, when I was still Qinglong's daughter. I'm guessing

I already had the same abilities that I do now, probably just stronger.

And then, because I believed myself human and without magic, it took this long for my magic to truly start coming back to me.

All of it fits.

"This is all true?" I ask at last.

Mr Sangong nods.

"Is my body...am I really alive? Am I human? What am I?"

Mr Sangong frowns, considering. "To be completely honest, I'm not entirely sure. You are both alive and you're not. Ilmu consumed your conscious memories, but your body will never forget the fact that for a time, it was dead. You will always carry death with you. Which might be part of your experience last night. Your body may have briefly been confronted with the memory of being dead and therefore tried to be dead once more. Or maybe it was you facing the void left behind by the loss of all your memories. I'm not sure."

"It felt like my body suddenly realised it had lost a limb."

"Then maybe it's a mix of both. I'm afraid I can't know for sure. This is beyond my knowledge. Even I have my limits." Mr Sangong gives a small smile.

"So am I human?"

"Your body is. The rest of you isn't."

"So my magic... I'm definitely not Touched."

"No. You appear to be, because of your mix of human and magic. But you are made of pure qi, which is why you are able to connect and talk to the spirit of all things."

"Wait, you can talk to me about what I am, now? I thought there was a spell in place to stop you."

"Because you already know. Qinglong didn't stop me

from saying specific words, she stopped Ilmu and I from revealing what you are to you. She didn't want us to say anything that would get back to the Guardians. Now that you know, we are both free to speak freely again..."

"Will they find out?"

"I don't know. There's a great deal I don't know about the Guardians. But it's very possible. What it will mean, again I don't know."

"Why did you help her? Qinglong? Isn't that dangerous, going against the other three Guardians?"

Mr Sangong looks down at his hands. "Because I understand the pain of losing a child. And I thought that she was right, that destruction isn't what will help us return to balance. Better to keep you whole than to add more destruction to the world. But it's become clear that you simply being back on earth hasn't helped restore balance. So I set about trying to get you to realise what you are—without telling you—in the hope that would help."

"Has it?"

Mr Sangong smiles. "I don't know, but things are certainly changing, aren't they?"

"And is that why you suddenly let me get into dangerous situations with the Mayak?"

"Yes. In the hope that when under sufficient pressure, some kind of survival instinct would kick in and help you access the truth of what you are."

"That was a pretty big gamble to take. What happens if my body dies—for real this time?"

"I'm not sure. I don't have all the answers."

It's odd to think of Mr Sangong just making it up as he goes along. I always thought of him as so incredibly wise, almost to the point of infallibility.

"What about Ilmu? She got banished for devouring my memories, didn't she?"

"Yes. The baku regularly audit each other in order to detect any signs of instability as early as possible. During one of her audits your memories were found, and they were identified as belonging to a high level Mayak, but one that they couldn't identify. Ilmu couldn't speak of it, so she was banished for having devoured Mayak memories without proper authorisation. I believe the banishment has been difficult for her to endure."

Maybe the fact that she was back with the other baku at the Great Mustering a couple of weeks ago means she has been forgiven? I'll have to ask her.

I look over to where Hunter is snoozing on the floor. "Speaking of which, she was the one who told me that Hunter is my guide. What is the connection there? Is Hunter truly a dog or is he something else?"

"Oh, he's a real dog."

"Then why is he my guide? Who made him like that?"

"Ilmu was extremely keen that you recover the truth of what you are. Once the truth about you comes out, her banishment will end since she did nothing wrong. So I think when you rescued Hunter she left something inside him that should have helped guide you."

"It didn't seem to do much, at least not until she had told me that he's my guide, and then he found the fish, but that's it."

Mr Sangong looks amused. "I don't think she expected him to be... Dogs are normally quite intelligent and receptive, but it appears Hunter was almost entirely impermeable to the knowledge she left inside him. The depth of your connection to him is probably a reflection of what Ilmu did, but I think she expected Hunter to take more of an active role in guiding you back to the truth of what you are. Instead...I don't think he did very much at all."

Hunter looks up at us, thumping his plumed tail. My gorgeous little failure. Not a failure at all, in fact. He got me there in the end — he just went about it in a completely Hunter-inefficient kind of way.

24

"There is one other thing that concerns me, Apiya," Mr Sangong says. "This thing with you and Sarroch, which almost resulted in Yue killing you..."

"There's nothing between me and Sarroch—he made that very clear. Yue's very jealous, and now I understand why. But I'm not...there's nothing there."

"In some ways Sarroch is very wise, as befits a being as old as he is. In others..." Mr Sangong shakes his head. "He is going to rather extreme lengths to see that you are safe."

"Extreme?"

Mr Sangong nods.

"What does that mean, extreme? What's he doing?"

"He is going beyond what is reasonable, and in so doing is stirring up trouble. This thing between you and Sarroch is problematic, Apiya."

"Wait, back up a second. Sarroch came and explained to me about Eyva, and how he doesn't want to be involved with anyone again. That he bonded to Yue so he wouldn't be available. He also felt responsible for Yue attacking me and wanted to make it right. That's just what he's doing—trying to make things right. I mean, he flat out told me that there could be nothing between us. "

It's a bit awkward, discussing this with Mr Sangong. I wonder if he knows about my crush on Sarroch and that whole embarrassing side of things. I hope not, but then I don't know how far Mr Sangong's powers extend. He might have known all along... Just the thought of it makes me cringe.

"Yes, and I'm sure he meant it. Sarroch is very good at lying to himself. But his actions don't match his words. Quite the opposite. And normally I wouldn't consider this to be any of my business. You and Sarroch are both free to do as you please. However, given the complexity of the situation with Yue, given who you are, and with everything else going on with the Mundanes...This isn't a good time for Sarroch to get his emotions tangled up, and so publicly. There are too many possible consequences with more ramifications than even I can keep track of."

Publicly? What the hell has he done? Or said? And what consequences?

Mr Sangong sighs. "Unfortunately the dice is already cast. We will have to see how it lands. If word of what went on with the Elders gets out, we will have a problem on our hands."

"What happened with the Elders? Does Yue know about it?"

"No. It was after she left."

She must know something, though, or have some inkling, maybe, of Sarroch's behaviour. That explains why she tracked me down wanting to know how I manipulated him.

"But what happened?" I ask. "What did Sarroch actually do or say?"

Mr Sangong gets up. "I think it's best if I keep that to myself. Things may not come to pass as I fear, in which case you do not need to know."

I bite down the urge to reply that my curiosity needs to know.

"But for now, Apiya, it would be best if you stayed away from Sarroch. Not that I expect it will make much difference, but if there is anything you can do to mitigate the situation, please do so."

The situation of Sarroch maybe having feelings for me that he himself doesn't recognise? Which apparently has all these consequences and ramifications, that I don't know about and don't understand?

"I'll do my best."

"Thank you."

After Mr Sangong leaves, I need a while to process everything.

If Mr Sangong was human I'd take it all with a pinch of salt, because it's easy to misinterpret the actions and emotions of another. But he's Mr Sangong which means he's probably right about Sarroch.

So what does that mean? Is Mr Sangong worried that Sarroch will lose it again like he did after Eyva died, or is it something else?

On second thought he can't be worried about that. Sarroch and Eyva were mated so it was completely different kettle of fish. Also I don't plan on dying.

However if Yue learns about this, my position—which is already not very secure—is about to get a whole lot more vulnerable.

And even if she doesn't, if Sarroch truly does have feelings for me, what are the chances I'll be able to fulfil my promise to Yue, and therefore keep her from attacking me again? Right now a snowball hurtling through seems to have a higher likelihood of success than me.

Yep, in short, things have just turned a whole lot more complicated.

Great.

At the same time, my stomach is fluttering with... excitement? Happiness? Nerves? At the thought that Sarroch might genuinely have feelings for me. Hard to tell what I feel exactly, and I don't want to delve too deeply into it.

In fact better to squash it down entirely.

I've made the error of inventing a flirtation once—I won't make the same mistake twice. Even if Mr Sangong is correct that doesn't mean anything will come to pass. Sarroch might never be willing to act on it. And if I go around thinking Sarroch has genuine feelings for me, I might be in danger of reciprocating, which then sets me right up for getting hurt when things inevitably go wrong.

Because they will.

So what I'm going to do is very simply ignore it all. Mr Sangong was probably right in not telling me the details— that makes it easier for me to stay at arm's length.

* * *

YOU'D THINK DISCOVERING THAT I AM THE DAUGHTER OF ONE of the Guardians of the sky, that I am in fact a being made of the very stuff that animates the whole world, would have earth-shattering, groundbreaking consequences.

That there would be a clear before and after. That my life would never be the same again. That all those around me would pick up on this change in me, and would act differently towards me.

"Open the kitchen tap for me."

"Tim, I'm busy."

"But I'm thirsty."

"You'll have to wait or drink out of your water bowl."

"Don't be ridiculous. I'm thirsty."

"Tim, I am the daughter of the Azure Dragon of the East. I'm able to connect with every creature on the planet, every object, and all their component parts. I have better things to do with my life than to turn on the kitchen tap for you every time you demand it. I will turn it on for you shortly, when I am finished with this."

"But I'm thirsty *now*."

And Tim begins to yowl the song of his people.

Clearly, as impressive as my new status is, it's not enough to impress my cat.

That was a Freudian slip. In fact, not a Freudian slip at all, just a slip of the tongue. Tim is not my cat. I do not take responsibility for him. I am very seriously considering throwing him out of my house — for all the good that would do, since he can come and go as he pleases.

I finally give up, throw my hands up in the air, and stomp over to the kitchen sink where I turn on the tap.

"There, that wasn't so hard, was it?" Tim asks before delicately leaning forward to take at the very most two sips of water.

"That's it?" I asked incredulously.

"I didn't say I was very thirsty. Geez, some people..." He jumps lightly off the counter and goes in search of a patch of sunlight in my courtyard.

I've cut back a chunk of the vines to let the sun through, but left enough that we now have a nice shaded area.

The feline-related interruption over, I return to what I was doing. Namely, writing Ilmu a lengthy message.

I'm following through with yesterday's resolution to ignore all that complicated business relating to Sarroch and Yue. I've got no idea what to do about any of it, and Mr Sangong is currently trying to figure out when and how it would be best to reveal who and what I am, given all that is going on. I'm just letting him get on with it.

Every so often Mr Sangong's voice rings in my head reminding me that Sarroch is getting his emotions tangled over me in public, and that he's not acting like an indifferent man. But every time I shut it up quickly and turn back to the one problem I've decided to focus on.

Namely, Ilmu not answering her phone.

I'm making a last ditched attempt at contacting her, and if I don't hear back, I'll ask Chai to take me to her office. Obviously it's now abundantly clear that I can't go out on my own any more—even I'm not so stupid and stubborn as to insist on that.

But I need to check on Ilmu. Make sure she's okay.

Maybe she's too busy to answer her phone. Maybe she doesn't want to talk to me for some reason.

Or maybe there's something else going on.

As if there wasn't enough going on already.

THE END FOR NOW

Now Available to pre-order:

HIDDEN BY JADE

The 5th book in the Razor's Edge Chronicles series by
Celine Jeanjean

WANT MORE?

Want to find out how Apiya met Chai, how she met Mr Sangong and started working at the barbershop?

Join the newsletter to receive Found by Rain, a prequel novella, for free.

Go to http://celinejeanjean.com/razor-bonus

ALSO BY CELINE JEANJEAN

If you want something to read in the mean time, you can dive into a whole new world that's like a mix of Victorian London and South East Asia. Discover a new cast of quirky characters, follow along their adventures and their banter, and escape into a **complete** 9 book series!

The gang's made up of:

- A skinny pickpocket with dreadlocks, a cheeky grin, and a smart mouth

- A foppish assassin with a fear of blood

- A handsome, elite fighter, master of the sardonic raised eyebrow

- A smuggler with a drinking problem and a propensity for brawling

- And a no-nonsense, heavily tattooed female machinist, trying to keep them all in line

Can they complete their missions without getting caught, killed, and without arguing?

The latter is by far the most problematic....

Check out the series over at http://celinejeanjean.com/viper-urchin/

Made in United States
North Haven, CT
07 January 2022

14279464R00107